The Company She Kept

MARJORIE ECCLES

The Company She Kept

St. Martin's Press ☙ New York

A THOMAS DUNNE BOOK.
An imprint of St. Martin's Press.

THE COMPANY SHE KEPT. Copyright © 1993 by Marjorie
Eccles. All rights reserved. Printed in the United States
of America. No part of this book may be used or
reproduced in any manner whatsoever without written
permission except in the case of brief quotations
embodied in critical articles or reviews. For information,
address St. Martin's Press, 175 Fifth Avenue,
New York, N.Y. 10010.

Library of Congress Cataloging-in-Publication Data

Eccles, Marjorie.
The company she kept : an Inspector Gil Mayo mystery /
by Marjorie Eccles.
p.   cm.
"A Thomas Dunne book."
ISBN 0-312-14297-8
1. Mayo, Gil (Fictitious character)—Fiction.
2. Police—England—Fiction.   3. England—Fiction.
I. Title.
PR6055.C33C65   1996
823'.914—dc20   96-3515   CIP

First published in Great Britain by The Crime Club,
an imprint of HarperCollins Publishers

First U.S. Edition: August 1996

10   9   8   7   6   5   4   3   2   1

The Company She Kept

CHAPTER 1

It wasn't until he was back in his room again, after eating in the hotel restaurant, that he opened the large envelope he'd been given when he checked in.

His first thought was that there'd been some mistake, although his name on the label, Mr F. Darbell, was spelled correctly. His second was that someone was fooling around with him: inside the envelope was a blue cardboard folder containing a sheaf of papers, apparently the manuscript of a novel, or at least part of one, entitled *The Carthage Affair*. Momentarily distracted by the title, Felix blinked and looked closer. There was no byline, but with a title like that it had to be either a thriller or a lurid romance of the sort written by women. He picked up the telephone and punched in the number of the reception desk.

He was answered by the manager. The envelope, it was reported after some inquiry, had been handed in earlier by a motorcycle messenger from a national express courier firm, and instructions given to the receptionist on duty that it had urgent priority and was to be delivered to Mr Darbell immediately he arrived.

'She must have made a mistake. It can't have been meant for me. Someone else with the same name?'

No, said the manager after a decidedly cool pause, she hadn't got the wrong person. Hardly likely with such an unusual name, was it, sir? And besides, his staff didn't make mistakes like that.

Felix asked if he might speak to the girl concerned, but she had just this minute gone off duty. The manager was politely sorry if it had inconvenienced Mr Darbell in any way, and if he wished he would get the girl to speak to him in the morning, but the implication was that he could in no way be personally responsible for his guests' correspondence . . . the question of the precise nature of the contents of the envelope hung rather delicately on the air but remained unanswered . . . if Mr Darbell felt there really had been a mistake he could perhaps bring the envelope down to the desk . . . ?

'If anyone inquires about it, it's here,' said Felix shortly. He was already undressed and in his Jaeger silk dressing-gown, and felt besides that the onus was on the person who'd made the slip-up. Very sure of his own rightness, he scarcely gave a second's consideration to the idea that the envelope might really have been meant for him.

He put down the receiver and shrugged the matter off. He'd done his part. If someone got to Darlington or Driffield or Drumnadrochit and found they were missing part of their novel . . . too bad. He'd more important things on his mind.

He'd had a light dinner, planning to spend the rest of the evening working in his room on the contract which was to be signed the next day. He worked for about half an hour, after which he pushed the papers aside, reluctantly admitting there was really no need for anything further. Although he'd planned to go through the contract minutely, making absolutely sure everything was tight as a drum, it was only one of those self-imposed tasks that made Lorna accuse him of being obsessive. There was really no fear that his staff hadn't performed with their usual efficiency; a leading firm of quantity surveyors such as his own didn't employ top people at top salaries to make a pig's ear of such things.

But having pushed the papers aside, he found himself restless. The trouble was, the title of that damned manuscript was going round and round in his brain. *The Carthage Affair.*

Felix swore, and crossed to the mini-bar, where he selected a miniature Scotch. He was careful about his alcohol consumption nowadays, and because he'd needed to keep a clear head for the meeting the next day he'd had no wine with his meal. He'd had several cups of strong black coffee afterwards though, specifically intended to keep him alert and awake while he worked. Which meant that just turning in and having an early night wasn't on. He'd never sleep if he did.

He stood at a loss in the middle of the bland, overheated, colour-coordinated room, the blue bedspread picking out the blue in the flowery curtains and the overstuffed armchair. Lorna's idea of good taste, right down to the innocuous flower prints. Feeling suddenly stifled, he tracked across the thick carpet to notch down the central heating, then turned the television on, switching from channel to channel but finding nothing that remotely interested him. The evening stretched before him, stale and profitless.

It was a long time since he'd let himself be thrown back on his inner resources and in lieu of anything better to do he flung himself down in the armchair, opened the case again and looked at the manuscript.

Felix had never been a great reader, especially not of fiction. He thought it a waste of the little free time he had to spare. He worked extremely hard and his leisure-time activities were a regular Friday night game of squash to keep himself in trim, plus weekend golf because the contacts made at the club came in useful. The last thing he wanted now was to read some trashy women's love story. On the other hand, the title was intriguing and it wasn't in him to sit twiddling his thumbs. He began leafing through it.

An hour later he looked up, rubbing his eyes. The mirror across the room showed him the same taut face with its high-bridged nose and pale blue eyes that he'd known for thirty-five years, now become the face of a stranger. Like a sleepwalker, he got himself another whisky and moved back into the armchair, where he sat staring into space. He hadn't quite finished the manuscript yet, but he didn't need to. It read like a story to which he already knew the dramatic ending: this was no piece of fiction as he'd thought at first. All the details were there, all the leading players, although the names and places had been thinly disguised.

There was also the command, right at the end. Just three terse lines.

Controlling his anger, he re-read it right through once more before he eventually climbed into bed, but he was destined not to sleep much that night. It was impossible to tell himself that it was just an uncanny coincidence. The writer had known too much, had too many of the details right. But it was equally impossible to believe that one of them, one of the group, would have acted in this way, suddenly, out of the blue, or even at all. He had known them well enough to be able to believe that. Surely, even after fourteen years, he could have counted on that?

Tossing and turning in the unfamiliar bed, he chewed over the problem. Which of them had known he was to be here tonight? Someone had. Realizing that only brought a boiling rage, knowing he'd been watched and followed for days, months, even years, the chance to play this sick joke waited for. And why? Why now, after all this time, had the sworn silence been broken?

It wasn't until dawn that he finally fell into an exhausted sleep, dreaming as he hadn't dreamed for years, nightmares of the sort he used to have when it all came back, when he saw again with terrifying clarity the prone figure at the bottom of the stairs on the sheeny flagstones of the big hall, and himself standing over it, knowing that his life, with everything in front of him a moment before, was finished.

He woke late, the aftertaste of the whisky sour in his mouth, dismissed with a shudder the idea of breakfast and showered and shaved hurriedly. He was struggling with his recalcitrant cufflinks—an expensive pair in some sort of dark, polished stone which were a present from Lorna that

he wore only occasionally in the interests of domestic har-
mony—when the telephone rang.

It was the receptionist who'd handed him the envelope.
She was sorry about the mix-up but was absolutely certain
it had been intended for him. There was no way she could
have confused him with any other of the hotel guests.

Swallowing his pride, Felix was forced to admit that he
was the one who had made the mistake, that he had eventually realized the envelope had been intended for him all
along. He apologized for jumping the gun. The receptionist,
a girl with a sunny nature, told him it didn't matter a bit,
no problem.

Before leaving his room, he had rung his secretary, a new
acquisition who was very much aware of her own efficiency.
Yes, there had been a few calls the previous day, among
them one from his solicitor.

'They wanted to get in touch with you urgently on a
personal matter, so I gave them the name of your hotel.
Did they contact you, Mr Darbell?'

'In a manner of speaking.'

He resisted the impulse to shake her out of her smug
complacency by telling her she'd no business to give his
whereabouts to anyone before checking their right to know,
not even his solicitor: in fairness to her, the lines *had* been
buzzing between them lately over matters concerning the
purchase of the new house. What upset him more was the
fact that whoever had arranged for the envelope to be
delivered had known even this.

He got through the morning somehow. The contract was
eventually signed with affability all round but he declined
lunch in the directors' dining-room and after snatching a
hurried snack at a local pub, drove the Jag fast through
intermittent driving rain towards the M6 and London. He
hadn't consciously taken the decision to leave the motorway
but when he reached Spaghetti Junction just after four and

peeled off, he knew it had been there all along. He stopped and used the car phone. Lorna sounded mildly disappointed that he wouldn't be home that night after all, but not overly so; she never did on these occasions. He suspected she was sometimes rather relieved. Whether she was or not, however, his compulsion to revisit the place where it had happened was overwhelming.

He avoided going through the wrought-iron gates and up the drive. It was too fraught with the memory of the last time he'd walked it, in the reverse direction. Still less did he want sight of the lake, glassy dark and deep near the little island at the centre, with reeds waving at the edges, and the broken-down old boathouse at the far end. He stood instead on the knoll above the road and saw as much as he wanted to see.

The ancient house, Flowerdew it was called, had sunk even further into dilapidation, although it had always had a weatherbeaten charm—in some ways rather like old Kitty herself, though not so bizarre. The monstrous extension, being newer, was in better shape than the rest and in consequence stuck out even more incongruously than he remembered, like a garden-party hat on a tweedy country lady of uncertain age.

The light was fading fast and another downpour threatened, but the willows were bare at this time of year and even from where he stood he could see the loose shutter on the old part of the house, the missing roof tiles, a crumbling of one of the twisted chimney stacks. The now sodden garden had all but reverted to nature. Brambles and bindweed ramped lawlessly over the flowerbeds, the old roses that she had so loved—*Cuisse de Nymphe, Céleste, Souvenir de la Malmaison*—sprawled and lolled intemperately over one another. He noticed that the holly hedge he and Tommo had trimmed when it was a mere four foot high had grown into an impenetrable fifteen-foot thicket, while the splendid line of Irish yews mourned the house's past with their shaggy, dipping, untrimmed branches. It must have been empty for a long time, nobody could possibly want to buy an old white elephant like Flowerdew, but at the thought of trying to get in and stirring old ghosts, his nerve gave out and he began to scramble down to the road again. It had been a mistake to return here instead of doing straight away what he had come to Lavenstock to accomplish.

Yet so real was his image of Flowerdew as it had been that even as he turned away he almost fancied he saw a faint movement in the air, an imagined wisp of smoke issuing from one of the chimneys or the flutter of a curtain, and for a moment quite thought he had conjured up some spirit, some genie from a bottle. And for a foolish, heart-constricting space, had the illusion she must still be there, that Kitty, against all the odds, was still alive.

CHAPTER 2

Mayo would never have noticed the letter if it hadn't been for the fancy deckle-edged writing paper, shading from palest shell pink, through rose-colour to near-fuchsia. He wouldn't have seen it anyway if he hadn't popped into the CID room on his way to the morning discussion with the Super. It had been a mistake to turn aside from the stern path to the Upper Chamber. Whenever he did he invariably got nobbled by somebody. In this case it was a flutter of pink among the mundane piles of official forms and buff folders on Detective-Sergeant Moon's desk that caught his eye, like a frivolous piece of female underwear in an army surplus store.

'Billy-doo from one of your admirers, Abigail?'

Abigail Moon responded with a warm smile, nice girl that she was. But then, Detective Chief Inspector Gil Mayo was also her boss and Abigail wasn't stupid. 'Chance'd be a fine thing, wouldn't it, sir?'

Transferred from the adjoining division of Hurstfield, newly made up to sergeant, she was the latest addition to his team, a young woman with a vivid face and a heavy mass of wavy hair, the colour of Oxford marmalade, which she wore drawn back into a thick plait when on duty. Marked out as a high flyer and with a university degree which didn't impress him half as much as her level-headed, commonsense approach to the job, she was still regarded warily, and in some cases with resentment, by those she was bound to by-pass. But she was earning their respect because she mucked in, could take a joke and never expected concessions because of her sex. Most of them approved of her anyway as a decorative addition to a department not noted for pretty faces—young Jenny Platt, the only other female CID member, excluded.

Instead of leaving it circumspectly at that and going on his way with a smile and a nod, Mayo perched his bulk on the edge of Abigail's desk. Big, powerful and authoritative, fit and brown from a recent walking weekend, he picked the letter up and ran his eyes down it. Out of idle curiosity, he lifted the sheet of paper to his nose, from the look of it expecting it to be as vilely-scented as it was highly-coloured. But he could only detect a faint echo of perfume, as if picked up from a scent bottle in a drawer or a handbag, rather than having been purposely impregnated. Or perhaps it was Abigail's scent he had caught, delicate, subtle and infinitely preferable either to the waves of DC Farrar's *Eau Sauvage* which usually pervaded the CID room first thing in the morning, or the *parfum de nicotine* from George Atkins's detestable pipe.

But neither Farrar nor Inspector Atkins were yet in this morning, the room's only occupants being the two sergeants, Moon and Kite. This didn't necessarily mean the rest of the CID were late: the non-uniformed branch's hours tended to be bizarre, a state of affairs that gave some of them a nervous breakdown or a reason to apply for a transfer back to uniform. On the other hand, one which suited some of the more fly types.

'Well, what's it supposed to be?' Mayo asked, mildly intrigued.

It was Kite who answered, flip as usual but without his usual grin. 'Believe that load of rubbish and you'll believe anything. Unsigned, unspecific, damn near unintelligible. One of *those*.'

The Sergeant, lanky and in his late thirties, was propping up the photocopier, or maybe it was propping him up. His normally open, friendly face looked drawn, his eyes tired, maybe from working too many late hours. Whatever it was, it was giving him grey hairs. His type of blond hair didn't show the grey easily—but surely it was lighter at the temples? Grey hairs, thought Mayo, and Kite seven years younger. God, that was depressing. People were soon going to be looking twice at what he'd always thought of as the distinguished sprinkle of silver in his own thick dark hair and wondering whether it wasn't time he retired.

'You'll see what he means when you read it, sir,' Abigail suggested, dispelling unwelcome thoughts.

Mayo was on Kite's side in the matter of anonymous communications, in so far as he'd no time either for anybody who wasn't prepared to put their name to what they wrote. On the other hand, anonymous tip-offs were a necessary evil to be accepted, even encouraged, with grateful thanks and without too many questions as to their provenance. Even though they were invariably from amateur informers, written out of spite, or a desire to get their own back, to shop somebody who'd done them wrong.

This one differed from the usual run in that it was not only disconnected and incoherent but also, as Kite said, non-specific. It began without preamble: '*The night she died Dido came. Dido Elissa. There were bad vibes that night. And*

Death for the old woman. She made out she was old and useless but could see everything without glasses and ears like a bat. The horrible red room. Babies' cremation urns. And the mask of Tanit wife of Ba'al. All-powerful. Death.' The text at this point was interrupted by a line of drawings, the same figure repeated again and again, a triangle surmounted by a circle bisected by two extended arms, in what appeared to be a crude representation of the female form. '*She would not have died if she had stayed away from England. If he had kept his temper. I have kept my mouth shut for fourteen years and said nothing but I was wrong. Murder must be punished.*'

It was not signed.

'See what I mean?' asked Kite as Mayo came to the end of this missive, turned the page over to see if there was anything more, but found nothing. 'Dido, Elissa—babies' cremation urns! What in the name of God are we expected to make of that?'

'Dido as in *Dido and Aeneas*,' Mayo was able to inform them modestly, enlightenment having gradually dawned on him as he read.

Kite, however, looked blank and Abigail, who might have known what Mayo meant but had learned to be careful of appearing too clever, said nothing.

'It's an opera. Maybe somebody saw it in London like I did, the other week. Over-stimulating to the imagination —that particular production at any rate.'

'Oh, an opera,' said Kite.

'Based on the legend of Dido, a queen of ancient Carthage, who ended up flinging herself into the flames when her lover Aeneas deserted her.'

Abigail couldn't resist that. 'What man on earth's worth that, I ask myself.' Her laugh almost took the acid out of it.

'She was also known as Elissa,' Mayo said, tapping the letter. 'And Tanit was the moon-goddess of Carthage who demanded sacrifices of babies and small children.'

'Sounds like a real fun evening!' Kite said.

'Disappointing.'

Mayo had gone alone and was glad he had. Purcell wasn't much in Sergeant Jones's line. Alex and he shared their intimate moments when their off-duty coincided and would, if he had his way, share the rest of their lives, but the one area where their tastes didn't coincide was music. She liked hers soft and easy and could take it or leave it, whereas for him it was serious and at the centre of his life. The tragic opera had been memorable for more than the felicitous marriage of words and the most glorious musical instrument of all, the human voice. It had been a clever, arty production, a combination of opera and dance, and a horrifying subtext which had underlined the dark themes of superstition and betrayal and sacrifice. With its dramatic background of flames and fire, and frenzied, naked dancers, he had found it ultimately deeply depressing. It had haunted him, if that wasn't too strong. At any rate, made the hairs rise on the back of his neck . . . just as this letter did.

He read it again and could make nothing of it. He decided it was probably from some poor soul who wasn't quite right in the head, or from someone who was having them on, with long odds on the latter. He'd learned to be cynical about these things.

Abigail said, 'What shall we do about following it up, sir?'

'What *can* we do, where do we start, without anything more specific to go on? There's no way this can be taken as material evidence of a murder. Even if we're expected, as I assume we are, to believe that years ago some old woman was murdered?'

She didn't appear to be too convinced, obviously believing there was some mileage in pursuing the idea. Her mouth was stubborn even though she knew he was watching her, judging her with the steady dark look that was capable of making potential suspects buckle at the knees. His gut feeling where Abigail was concerned was that she was good, and going to be better. She was young and as far as he knew had no ties or encumbrances, which was all to the good as far as her career was concerned. Tough going stimulated her; throw down a challenge in front of her and she'd pick it up and run with it—more than some of her male colleagues were prepared to do. But he thought briefly of last month's crime figures, this month's budget, his permanently overstretched team, shook his head and then dismissed the letter from his mind.

He flicked the pink paper back on to the desk. 'Nasty overtones—but why stop there? If she really has something to tell, she'll write again. I doubt it, though, now that she's got it off her chest.'

Abigail looked enigmatic at his choice of pronoun, but it hadn't only been the pink scented paper and its matching envelope, lined with deepest rose, that was suggestive of a woman writer. There was also—he had to say it—the hysterical tone. And the handwriting, which was loopy and irregular, increasingly illegible towards the end, with backward-curling down-loops and sentences only half-completed. And the erratic syntax and punctuation, which *could*, of course, apply to either sex. But the general tone of the letter struck him as unquestionably female.

He went on his way at last, certain they had heard the end of the whole thing. A prediction which could hardly have been more wrong.

CHAPTER 3

When Sophie first came to Flowerdew in 1978, a sepia photograph had stood on the walnut lowboy in the drawing-room: a snapshot of Kitty Wilbraham when young, a small but gallant figure in a safari jacket and divided skirt, wearing a pith helmet with a wealth of richly curling hair tumbling from under it. Around her were the stone ruins of Carthage, beside her a monumental fallen column, its mighty head in the dust. Two men were pictured with her. One of them was her husband, Alfred, a stout, bearded, elderly figure reminiscent of King George the Fifth, and clad—inexplicably under that bright harsh sun—in tweed plus fours and a stiff collar. The other man was Miloslav Bron, another archæologist who had been working with the Wilbrahams on the same dig. He was taller than Alfred, and very dark, sporting a bold moustache, a regrettable shirt and a louche smile. But then he was, after all, a foreigner.

The departed Alfred Wilbraham seemed to have been an unimpeachably virtuous figure whose integrity, erudition and wisdom Kitty never ceased to extol. He had died in Tunisia from a fall of rock upon his unprotected head after an inexplicable failure to keep to his own rules and wear a helmet when working. He left no issue but to Kitty he had willed Flowerdew, a largeish house about a dozen miles from Lavenstock, named for the Elizabethan adventurer who had built it. The place had belonged to Alfred's family for generations and was shabby through a continued lack of interest in spending money on its maintenance. It was also extremely inconvenient by modern standards, but he hoped she would continue to use it as a retreat in the intervals of grubbing about in the sand.

Kitty, Sophie gathered when she began to piece the bits of her life together, had done as Alfred wished and kept the house as her base whenever she was in England with the exception of the war years, when she had enlisted in the ATS in the hope of being sent abroad. In view of her intimate knowledge of the Middle East, however, she was immediately put on to secret work at the War Office, where she was kept for the duration. Obliged to make the best of it, she worked off her ferocious energy in the little spare time she had by writing books about her work on the excavations of Carthage, which were published with some success after the war. Not even the publicity this brought her (which she was not slow to play up to by adopting a flamboyant style of dressing) could keep her permanently from her life's work in Tunisia, however. When the flush of fame had died down she returned there, until age and arthritis forced her to retire permanently to Flowerdew. She put on weight, grew more bizarre than ever, drank quantities of sweet mint tea all day long and became obsessed with the idea that she was about to die and that she must write her memoirs before she did.

It would give her something to occupy herself with, she announced and besides, the money would come in useful. Flowerdew had never recovered from its sad neglect before and during the war; it had now reached the age where it was threatening to fall into complete ruin if it were not propitiated by having vast sums of money spent on it. Money didn't have the same value as it had when Alfred died; she was growing poor. Nobody believed this. Alfred had left her what was a comfortable fortune by any standards but, open-handed in other directions, she was certainly canny with money.

Writing had always come easily to Kitty and despite her belief in her imminent demise the flow was unstemmed. She had a trained mind well-honed by her days at Girton, her notes had always been meticulously kept and arranged, she had an excellent memory and she was blessed with a prose style that was sharp and entertaining and not at all what might have been expected from her dusty subject. Her lightness of touch was frowned upon by other academics —*Funerary Customs and Sacrificial Rites in Phœnician Carthage*, the title of her latest book, and the Punic Wars, in which field she was an acknowledged expert, were after all no laughing matter—although no fault could be found with her scholarship. They were only jealous, Kitty retorted, because her books continued to sell well. And not only as textbooks for serious students but to armchair archæologists who preferred to take their doses of culture sweetened by a little lightness and humour.

When it came to her memoirs, however, it became apparent that Kitty's normal exuberance and enthusiasm would need to be leavened with circumspection. Her personal life had been enlivened by encounters and friendships with all sorts and conditions of people; she had met princes and potentates and what she had to tell was quite often scandalous, sometimes libellous, and would certainly not be well received in the touchy climate of Middle Eastern politics. Even she began to realize that she must cut and prune and omit where necessary, something that went so much against the grain of her own nature that she began to lose interest in the idea.

It was Madeleine Freeman who suggested she employ a secretary. Madeleine was Kitty's doctor, a sensible and dedicated young woman whose advice was always sound, but it was only because arthritis was beginning to make it difficult to hold a pen or bang away on her typewriter without a good deal of pain that Kitty finally gave in.

Irena immediately came to mind as a candidate for the job: she was reasonably intelligent, had time on her hands —and she also owed Kitty a great deal. Intimating that she had been one of the political dissidents who had fled Czechoslovakia in the disillusioned years following the Prague Spring, she had descended without warning on Flowerdew six months previously. Her foot once in the door, she stayed, infuriating Jessie Crowther by invading her kitchen to cook heavy Slovak dishes, and upsetting the peaceful tenor of Kitty's life with all the Central European drama and temperament brought into it. She appeared to have settled in permanently, with no desire to find herself paid employment.

Why didn't Kitty send her packing?

'But she's Milo's daughter!' she said, when asked. 'I owe him that, at least. And—' clinching it—'Alfred would have wished it.' Besides, anyone could see that mixed with her exasperation was a reluctant affection for the gauche, clumsy, unattractive woman Irena was.

But whatever she felt about her, Kitty was adamant that she wouldn't do as a secretary: she was too excitable and unreliable, and just as likely to put down her own wild interpretation of events if such a thing happened to occur to her. A woman of her age, pushing forty, should be capable of keeping her mouth shut, but Irena was not. And there were some things, Kitty hinted, it was better she shouldn't know about yet, possibly never.

Felix she wouldn't consider, either, though he too was hanging around the house at present with nothing to do but help Tommo in the garden while waiting to go up to his university, a refugee from his parents' broken marriage to whom she had given temporary lodging. For one thing, Felix was a young man of no imagination and would be shocked at some of the things she had to tell; his self-protective good manners would prevent him remarking on what he learned—but possibly not from trying to make capital of it later. He was clever and already had a definite eye to the main chance, though you couldn't altogether blame him for that, poor boy. It came of having that dreadful pushy mother.

The one person Kitty would really have liked to work with her was Madeleine, but as a recently qualified and newly-appointed junior partner in the local medical practice, she was much too busy to ask.

'You'll have to advertise,' said Jessie Crowther, putting her practical Yorkshire finger right on the button, as usual.

'I'll do no such thing!' declared Kitty. 'I want no strangers poking their noses into my affairs.' Jessie, who'd been Kitty's housekeeper for thirty years, said nothing, and waited. A few days later Kitty inserted her advert in the local paper.

What she wanted, she had decided, was someone who would enter into the spirit of the thing, yet know where to draw the line. Someone decisive and perhaps even a little bossy, who wouldn't let her go too far. Someone ruthless where she was overflowing.

What she got was Sophie Amhurst.

'What a beautifully limpid creature you are!' were almost her first words to Sophie, when Jessie had conducted the girl through the rather spooky house towards the hooded basket chair in the garden where Kitty sat enthroned like an empress. And Sophie at eighteen, though not at all sure what this fat, bizarrely-dressed old woman with the lively dark eyes meant, decided to take it as a compliment—though how much better it would have been if the words had been juxtaposed: if she'd said 'limpidly beautiful' rather than the other way round.

'I just happened to see your ad and thought it might be fun,' she replied naïvely when Kitty asked what had made her apply, and indeed it could easily have happened that way. But the truth was that it had been Roz who had seen the advert and thought the job would be good experience for Sophie. Sophie had just left school and had decided she was never, ever, ever going to make plans, she was sick of being pushed around and was henceforth going to live spontaneously, be a truly free spirit. To which Roz retorted that was an assumption that depended on leaving other people to do the planning, otherwise the world would be in chaos. Roz, filled with practical common sense, liked her life to be ordered and disciplined; she'd taken responsibility for Sophie ever since their parents died. Despite her degree, she was engaged to be married to a policeman.

But whatever Roz thought, Sophie knew it was her own decision to apply for the job. Flowerdew, or something like it, though she had never seen the house until she went along for the interview with Mrs Wilbraham, had always been there on the edges of her imagination, something like it had always featured in the distant landscape of her romantic mind. Its very name conjured up for her a kind of enchantment. Camelot's færy mythic towers, Avalon, Morte d'Arthur . . . the heady stuff of legend and romance.

What had clinched the decision to apply, however, had been the fact that the Mrs Wilbraham who needed a secretary was a writer. A little disappointing to find, on inquiry at the library, that she was a writer of archæological textbooks, but no matter. Sophie had decided some time ago that writing was to be her metier. She didn't need the money, their parents had left her and Roz dangerously free of the necessity to work for their living, but all her friends were deciding on careers and it seemed to her that being a writer sounded interestingly different and was just the thing to give her the untramelled lifestyle she so longed for. Without, of course, too many restrictions on her time or too much hard work. She'd learned to type, though somewhat erratically, and although she didn't yet know what she wanted to write about, this opportunity to pick up a few hints was too good to miss. Something must surely rub off on her!

If Kitty was thrillingly like Sophie's conception of a writer, with a rich silk scarf wound low on her forehead, her exotic jewellery and her rather grubby rubbed silk caftan embroidered with tarnished silver thread, Sophie was not at all what Kitty had envisaged. Thin, brown-haired and lightly-boned, she sat poised on the edge of her chair as if about to take wing, her clear hazel eyes filled with a gentle dreaminess, large and intelligent as the eyes of a deer. Following that bright expressive gaze, Kitty saw it fixed on the not too distant figure of Tommo, clearing pondweed from between the waterlilies at the edges of the lake— Tommo, dark and secretive, inscrutably keeping his own counsel, who had come to live in the cottage in the grounds under his own terms: handyman work around the house and garden in exchange for accommodation, a small wage and no questions asked about his personal life. Yet Kitty envisaged no trouble to come. True, the girl was young and doubtless impressionable and there were two presentable young men around the place, but Tommo was Tommo, and Felix—well, pooh, he wouldn't be the type to appeal to Sophie! Kitty had conceived an immediate liking for the girl and felt an empathy between them strong enough to decide to set her on, without even bothering to ask her about her qualifications.

'That's it, then. I hope you like mint tea.'

'I've never had it,' said Sophie honestly, thinking it sounded gruesome, 'but I'll try anything once.'

'That's the spirit! I can see you're a person after my own heart. We're going to get on splendidly!' Kitty beamed, and was rewarded by an answering smile that Sophie herself felt to spring from her very heart. She took all this to mean she was engaged, and hoped her typing would be up to it.

As for Kitty, she had no qualms. She knew instinctively that Sophie would fit in very well with the rest of the bright young people who had come in various ways to surround her and who made her feel as she had when she, too, was young, in her twenties, at Cambridge, a most luminous star in all that brilliant firmament. Before she had met and married Alfred Wilbraham. Or before her beloved Alfred had met, married and made her what she was.

CHAPTER 4

The second Tuesday in March began for Mayo, after a mere three hours' sleep, with a puncture. As a consequence, he arrived late and in a bad temper at his desk at Milford Road Divisional Headquarters only to find that a material witness in the squalid child-pornography case he and Kite had been winding up had done a disappearing act. From then on, it was downhill all the way.

It was a foul day. Dark and rainy, the lights on all day. At ten p.m, having just finished interrogating another of the witnesses in the case with Kite—one who'd been acting like the three wise monkeys for three hours and who'd then suddenly decided to break his *omertà*—and having read the man's statement and filed his own report, Mayo sent Kite off home.

'Call it a day, Martin.' He stretched, walked to the window and peered out into the rainy darkness. 'Sheila will be wondering whether she has a husband at all.'

'I'll be off then, if you say so,' Kite replied, unusually compliant.

'You all right, Martin?'

'Shagged out, but I'll no doubt live! G'night then, see you in the morning.'

'Mind how you go,' Mayo said, watching the cars below slide like fish through an aquarium. 'I wouldn't turn a dog out in this weather.'

Neither of them had seen their beds yesterday until the small hours and now, tired to the point where nothing was making much sense any longer, he swept his own desk clear and followed Kite. He drove home through the rain-pelted streets, parked his car in the garage, fell over Moses, his landlady's cat, and found a letter waiting for him from his daughter, Julie, who was en route to Australia, having jettisoned her catering course in favour of learning about life. He worried and fretted over his motherless child as only a father can, imagining her in the sort of perilous situations only a policeman would. The measure of his exhaustion was that he decided reading the letter could wait until the morning.

He had a shower, the stinging hot water succeeding in washing away the tension and partially clearing his mind.

He was morosely viewing the uninspired contents of his fridge and wondering whether he could be bothered to eat or not before bed, when the telephone rang. In his present mood he was ready to contemplate not answering it but his flatmate, Bert the parrot, wished on him by Julie for the duration of her travels, had other views. In several misguided moments, Alex had taught him to shout 'Shop!' every time the phone rang. Bert had quickly reached the peak of his learning curve, but this had proved no bar to his strong streak of exhibitionism. Ignoring him made no difference. In the end Mayo had to answer the phone in self-defence.

It was Kite. 'Sorry about this. We have a body. Woman found by a lorry-driver in a lay-by on Hartopp Moor. I'm there now and I've done all the necessary, contacted the coroner's officer and so on. Doc Ison's here and Timpson-Ludgate's on his way.'

'Right, Martin, I'll be as quick as I can.'

After pulling on his clothes and downing a cup of black coffee in the hope of getting the adrenalin going again, Mayo manœuvred his car out of the garage and started up with as little noise as possible in order not to wake Miss Vickers and her brother, both of them seventy-plus and light sleepers.

The wipers sluiced the torrential rain across the windscreen, the wet road stretched like an oil slick before him as he slid round the base of the hill that led up on to the moor. Seven miles from Lavenstock and it might have been on the moon, a desolate landscape with nothing for miles except bare hills, a few stunted trees and outcrops of rock.

Rounding the corner of the hill, he came to the police 'Slow' signs and a scene familiar to him from dozens of other occasions: beetle-like figures scurrying about in shining wet capes, the temporary lighting revealing a clutch of police cars, a scenes-of-crime van, plus a huge multi-wheeled low-loader truck with a Birmingham registration number pulled in to the lay-by. The pathologist had beaten him to it; his vintage Rover was parked behind Doc Ison's car and the truck. Headlights suddenly sliced the darkness as several cars coming the other way swept into view, slowing and craning to see what was going on before being waved irritably on by one of the caped figures.

Martin Kite came forward to meet him as he got out of his car. 'Over here, sir.'

The Sergeant led him behind a mass of red sandstone outcrop that jutted out from the moorland, where plastic screens had been rigged to provide a rough shelter and Ison and the pathologist were waiting for Sergeant Napier, crouched underneath it, to finish with his cameras. Both men looked up and grunted a greeting, the pathologist's normally cheerful and rubicund face morose under a dripping fisherman's hat.

The rain drummed on to the plastic as Mayo ducked under it. A woman's body lay on the sedge, one leg in a stiletto-heeled shoe lying at a grotesque angle. Prepared as he was for the sight, his gorge still rose, his stomach tightening into its accustomed knots. Death had not been merciful. He looked down at her with pity. However attractive she'd once been, she now looked repulsive, her face congested and bloated, the bruises on her throat making an obvious statement. Most of the make-up she'd worn had been washed off by the rain, leaving only the sticky-looking lipstick intact, a ghastly slash of scarlet across the naked, cyanosed face. A slackness under the chin revealed her as no longer young, the hanks of bleached hair were soaked with rain, its darker roots pitifully revealed. There was no dignity in this sort of death: the short skirt was ruckled up above the thighs, the tights and red silk knickers half pulled down.

The photographers had finished and the doctors were preparing to examine the body. Mayo hunched his coat collar further round his neck and backed out into the rain to give them room, motioning Kite to join him. 'Do we know who she is?'

'Not yet. No handbag, nothing in the pockets, but she'll be identifiable, won't she?'

'More easily than most.'

For even the blueing of the face hadn't hidden the birthmark, the port-wine stain down the side of her face. That was probably the reason she'd worn her hair long, to cover it, but anyone meeting and talking to her would have been bound to have noticed it and remembered her.

'Poor wench.' Kite's glance went back in the direction of the body. 'Occupational hazard, but that doesn't make it any better, does it? Terrible thing to happen to any woman.'

The situation was familiar: the thick lipstick, the dyed hair, the short skirt and sexy underwear spoke for themselves. It was an easy enough assumption that she'd been on the game, a woman who took known risks and had ended up like many of her sisters before her; unaccountably, the easy conclusion jarred. The clothes, for one thing, wet through though they were, didn't look cheap, although that in itself meant nothing: she might have been a high-class tart. And the earring she wore—one earring only, mind. Quality there. Ornately worked silver studded with coloured stones, might be worth something. Mayo looked again at the naked, blemished face. 'Let's try to keep an open mind.'

Kite threw him a swift glance and the velcro on his waterproof came apart with a tearing sound as he fished for a handkerchief to wipe his face. 'It was the lorry-driver found her. He's on his way home to Birmingham, stopped here to relieve himself and stumbled across her is what he says.' He jerked his head towards the lorry, where the driver could be seen slumped over the wheel, his head resting on his arms. 'There's a pub half a mile back—couldn't turn his vehicle here, so he walked back and knocked them up to ring us. His cab phone's on the blink.'

'I'll have a word. Meanwhile, see nobody goes putting their size twelves where they shouldn't,' Mayo instructed. 'When the medics have finished we'll let as many as we can go home and get a spot of shut-eye, then we'll make a search at first light.' It was counter-productive to thrash around in the dark, possibly obliterating beyond hope anything that might be useful. Daylight and hopefully a better day would improve the chances a hundred per cent. 'Though what we're going to find after all this is anybody's guess,' he said to his sergeant, as Kite went off to issue his own orders.

Mayo waited until another car had swished past and then ran, head down, to open the door of the lorry and swing himself up into the steamed-up cab, on to the seat next to the driver.

Rubbing his eyes and yawning, the driver raised his head. 'Sorry, mate, couldn't keep my eyes open any longer, I'm just about knackered.' He blinked and said blearily, 'Oh, you're not the Sergeant.'

'Detective Chief Inspector Mayo. I hear you found the body. Tell me about it, will you?'

'What, again? Give me a break! It's not exactly a picnic driving to flaming Poland and back with a load of heavy boilers, mate!'

'I'm sorry, but it can't be helped.'

The driver glanced at the politely implacable face next to him, reached for his cigarettes and lit up. 'Not my day, is it? If I hadn't been pushing it to get home I wouldn't still have been on the road and run into this here how-do.'

'What are you doing on this road at all if you're in such an almighty hurry? Been a lot quicker on the motorway.'

'Heard further back there's been a big pile-up south of Coventry, so I made up my mind to miss it—and where d'you think all this other traffic's coming from?'

'Fair enough.'

The driver's name was McKinley, a Brummie Irishman

employed by a firm of heavy haulage contractors. He was a huge hunk of a man, unshaven, with great muscular tattooed arms and a big belly. A lonely life these drivers led, on the road for days, sometimes weeks, at a time.

'You didn't pick her up somewhere, did you?'

The driver gave Mayo back look for look, while the rain went on belting down on the cab roof. 'No, mate, I bloody didn't. She was there when I went round the back of that there rock for a run-off.'

'What time was that?'

'Around eleven, I reckon. Soon as I found her I walked back to that pub and asked them to ring you. I'd hardly have bothered with that if I'd done for her, would I?'

He hadn't troubled to dry his hair and he was steaming like a wet dog, and on the face of it, it was an unlikely scenario, but people overcome with guilt acted in strange and often totally inexplicable ways.

'People do funny things, you'd be surprised.'

'Well, not me, not that kind of funny. And I can do without them kind of remarks, thank you very much. I've a wife and kids and I'd like to be on my way home to them right now, if that's all the same with you. Holy Mother of God, I've seen some sights in my time, but that beats all!' The driver swallowed, wiped his hand across his mouth. 'I reckon you're used to it.'

'Not so's you'd notice,' Mayo said drily, his hand on the door. 'Thank you, Mr McKinley, I'll send somebody in shortly to take your statement.'

'How shortly?'

'As soon as possible. We're no more anxious than you are to stop out here.'

McKinley swore again. 'I need my head seeing to! I could've said nothing to nobody. I'm already running out of time. You keep me here much longer and it'll put the kybosh on me getting home. I'm not risking my licence, pushing on over the limits.'

'Very wise of you, but we shall have to detain you a bit longer before we let you go, Mr McKinley. And when we do, see that we know where to get in touch—don't make any more plans to go out of the country without letting us know.'

'Listen, I go when and where I'm sent—anybody'd think I was on a bloody package tour! I suppose it's too much to expect you lot to believe I'd nothing to do with this!' McKinley thrust his big red face pugnaciously towards Mayo.

Mayo could have told the driver he wasn't in the business of believing any one thing anybody told him, until it was proved otherwise in black and white, but he knew he might as well save his breath. He looked at the ham-like hands gripping the steering-wheel. One squeeze round a delicate throat . . .

Plunging out into the rain again, he made long strides towards the shelter, where the two medics were beginning to pack up their instruments.

'How long has she been dead?' began Timpson-Ludgate, anticipating the first, most important question. 'I can only give you an approximate time. Rigor's hardly begun. Not more than three or four hours, say between six and eight. You don't need me to tell you how she died, but wait for confirmation. Doesn't appear to have been sexually inter-fered with, though I'll be buggered how I'm expected to deliver pronouncements in conditions like this.' He sneezed several times into a large handkerchief, revealing a heavy cold as the source of his irritability. 'Tell you better tomorrow,' he added, with a finality that indicated nothing would persuade him to get on with the post-mortem before the morning.

'Somebody disturbed him, then?'

'How should I know that? I'm not omniscient. What I can tell you is, it's unlikely she was killed here. For one thing, as your Sergeant's pointed out, it doesn't look as though there's been a struggle. There's also a degree of hypostasis, blood draining to the lower parts, *post-mortem*. And I'll leave the deductions about that to you.'

Which was about as helpful as Mayo had expected. Brought here bundled in the boot of a car, most likely, and any tyre tracks would have been washed out in five minutes with the sort of rain that was coming down.

'If your photographers have got all you want, you can take her away now, we've finished with her for the moment. She's all yours,' Ison said. He and the pathologist watched closely as the victim's feet and head were sealed into plastic bags, and then the hands, against the possibility she had fought with her attacker and that fragments of his skin might be under her nails. At the same moment as the body, now in its temporary coffin, was lifted into the waiting ambulance, the rain stopped with disconcerting suddenness and the clouds parted to reveal a full moon shedding an eerie light on to the men squelching around outside the cordoned-off area where the body had lain.

One of the dripping DCs approached Mayo, his dark hair plastered to his head. 'Could I have a word, sir?'

'Yes, Spalding, what is it?'

'I think I know who she might be . . .'

Mayo cast his dark look over the constable, a man he was never really sure he understood. A man who kept himself to himself, quiet and dependable, intelligent though apparently unambitious, still a constable and knocking on for forty. A bit of an enigma, all in all, though Mayo wasn't quarrelling with that. He didn't brandish the details of his own personal life around for public consumption, either.

'Haven't seen her for years,' Spalding went on. A raindrop slid down his nose and hung on the end. 'And in the state she's in, I wouldn't like to be categoric, but I think she's a woman called Angie Robinson.'

'Why didn't you say so before?'

Spalding didn't look very happy about having said so

now. 'Couldn't be sure, sir. It was only when we were lifting her—and her hair fell away from her face and . . .' He stopped to brush the raindrop off his nose.

'And you saw the birthmark. OK. Go on.'

'I might be wrong. I don't think I ever spoke to her more than a couple of times. She was just somebody my wife had met.'

He must be talking about his ex-wife. It was known that Nick Spalding was another recent casualty of the police force, one whose marriage hadn't survived the stresses and strains put on it. That much Mayo knew, but no more. 'Right. You'd better tell me what you know about her— and in what circumstances your wife knew her.'

'I wouldn't say Roz *knew* her, sir, she was only an acquaintance.' He was still reluctant to get involved. 'Roz and her sister got to meet her through the woman Sophie was working for at the time—some old woman who'd been a famous archæologist in her day and was writing her memoirs. Lived near Morwen, in a big old house called Flowerdew.'

'This sister, then—she should be able to tell us something about Angie Robinson?'

'If she's at home and in the right mood,' Spalding said shortly. 'And if she wants to talk about it. The old woman at Flowerdew suddenly decided she was going abroad, so Sophie's job there ended, and since then she's spent most of her time gadding about the world—in between divorces, that is.'

'Maybe it'd better be your wife we see first in that case.' Mayo decided he didn't much like the sound of this Sophie as a witness.

'Oh, I don't think so, sir,' Spalding said quickly. 'As I say, she didn't know Angie Robinson much more than I did.'

'We've got to start somewhere, man!'

'Yes, sir.'

'Let Sergeant Kite have her address. She's Mrs—?'

'It's still Spalding, sir. We're not divorced, only living apart,' Spalding said woodenly. 'She lives in Pennybridge.'

Pennybridge at eight in the morning was quiet and appealing, looking at its best in the morning sun, sharp after the night of rain. A picturesque village on the outskirts of Lavenstock whose charms had been the architect of its own downfall, it had attracted estate developers and caused the prices to soar of any old tumbledown cottage anywhere in the vicinity, and especially the period houses clustering round the green. As the well-off moved in, young village people left for flats and council houses in Lavenstock, and eventually the now upmarket village expanded so far it had become little more than a prosperous suburb of Lavenstock. It was the sort of place that brought out all Kite's Leftist tendencies but he kept his opinions to himself because Abigail refused to be wound up by them and was in any case obviously wrapped up in her own thoughts. Usually bright and chatty, she'd concentrated on her driving and had hardly had a word for the cat since they left Lavenstock. It suited Kite to let her drive; she'd had more than the three or four hours' sleep he and Mayo had managed to catch.

Roz Spalding lived in one of the new houses of neo-Georgian design in a small, select crescent just off the main street. There were only about half a dozen of them, set well back, their landscaped front gardens open plan. A small development, select and expensive, every one with at least four bedrooms and a double garage. A notice on a tree said a neighbourhood watch scheme operated here.

'No wonder old Spalding hasn't got married again,' Kite said, 'if his ex's tastes run to this! Must soak him dry, keeping her in this style.'

'She doesn't need money from him, she has plenty of her own. A house like this is peanuts to her.'

'How do you know?'

'Oh, word gets around,' Abigail said, unbuckling her seat-belt. 'Her old man was loaded, didn't you know? He and his wife were killed in that air crash over Belgium and everything went to Roz and her sister. Bet she could buy you out, ten times over.'

'That wouldn't take much,' Kite said. 'But now you mention it, I do remember hearing something about it. Come on, let's get this over with.'

Abigail said nothing more, but followed in his wake, reluctantly, albeit she had her own reasons for wanting the interview over as quickly as possible.

Roz Spalding turned out to be ordinary enough, a pleasant-faced, capable-looking woman in her late thirties with a sleek, short haircut. The house was comfortably, though by no means luxuriously, furnished, with toys and children's comics on the chairs and a smelly old dog to welcome them. No children were in evidence—only a photograph of a most beautiful child, a boy of about six or seven, with his mother's fair hair and Spalding's dark eyes.

Kite apologized to Mrs Spalding for disturbing her, though they were here at this hour at her request, since she had said on the phone she had to be out of the house by nine-thirty. He noticed books, papers and a small personal computer were spread over the surface of a large table in front of the window.

'Angie Robinson?' she repeated. 'That's a name I haven't heard for years!'

Kite said, 'A woman has been found dead and we've reason to believe it may be her. We want someone to confirm this and we've been told you knew her.'

'Dead, Angie? Good heavens, was it an accident?'

'I'm afraid the woman we're trying to identify has been murdered, Mrs Spalding,' he said.

'What?' Her eyes widened in shock. 'Well, yes, I did know her, but as I said, it was years ago, and even then she wasn't much more than an acquaintance. What made you come to me? No, don't tell me, it was Nick who put you on to me!' Her cooperative attitude changed abruptly and she became uptight and close-lipped. 'He'd no right to do that! In any case, it's so long since I saw her, I doubt if I'd recognize her.'

'If it's the same person,' Kite began, 'she had a distinctive birthmark . . .'

'I'm sorry, I can't help you.'

'Your sister, Sophie—'

'No! You mustn't ask Sophie!' As if realizing that her voice had been needlessly sharp, she added lamely, 'She hardly knew her, either.'

'We're not asking either of you to identify her, Mrs Spalding. Only to know if you can tell us who can.'

'Sorry, I know you're only doing your job.' She thought for a moment then said, 'The best person would be Madeleine Freeman—Dr Freeman.'

'The same Dr Freeman who's been in the *Advertiser* a lot recently about the Women's Hospital?' Abigail said, attempting to regain Roz Spalding's cooperation.

The other woman, hearing her speak for the first time, looked at Abigail as if her presence hadn't registered until then. And as she looked, her gaze intensified, her colour gradually heightened. Their eyes met and locked and Abigail's jaw began to ache with the effort of keeping her expression neutral and her eyes from straying to the photograph of the child. Damn! she thought, I should have left things as they were, melted into the background, I should have had the sense at least to keep my mouth shut.

'Really got the bit between her teeth about that, hasn't she—Dr Freeman?' Kite put in, looking from one woman to another and wondering what was up. That week's edition of the *Advertiser* had prominently displayed a photograph of Madeleine Freeman above yet another protest article about the decision to close the local Women's Hospital, a

small but revered and time-honoured institution that was
staffed entirely by women, for women.

'With good reason,' Roz Spalding said abruptly, drag-
ging her gaze from Abigail's face. 'The women of this town
need somebody like her to champion them.'

'Mm,' Kite mumbled wondering why he'd been so fool-
hardy as to embark on this particular voyage, which he'd
found to his cost was all too likely to be a stormy one.
He'd already had enough of it at home, having been unwise
enough to remark to his wife that he didn't see any reason
for keeping open a reputedly uneconomic unit when there
were equally good and easily accessible facilities at the
County, the town's main hospital.

'And where you're just as likely to be treated by some
man who basically has no idea what you're on about,'
Sheila had replied coldly.

After the sound of the police car engine had died away Roz
went back to the correspondence papers she was marking.
She had to have them finished ready for posting before she
drove up to the hospital anyway, and concentrating on
them would keep her mind off the last few minutes. She'd
grown used to bringing a fierce concentration to her work
lately. It helped, in some very small measure, to have at
least one tiny corner of her mind not entirely taken over by
the huge and all-encompassing pain, to feel that there was
something at least that she could do. It didn't always work
and today was one of those times. She told herself that she
had no right to be hurt by what had just happened, but
that didn't help, either. She pushed her chair back and
went to make herself some coffee.

Staring out of the window with her hands clasped round
the mug for warmth—her hands, like her heart, seemed
perpetually icy these days—she tried to picture Angie
Robinson, as she'd been all those years ago. Silly and totally
self-centred, teetering about on high, stiletto heels, always

patting and fiddling with that candy-floss bleached hair.
Tolerated, poor girl, but never liked. And convinced this
was because of the nævus on her face and not due to her
own nature—though where, Roz wondered now with the
greater charity of maturity, did one end and the other
begin?

What had she been doing since then, what had they all
been doing since Flowerdew? How long ago was it? Well,
Sophie had begun working there when she left school—it
must have been thirteen, or even fourteen, years . . .

CHAPTER 5

When she first started work at Flowerdew, Sophie had
found that Kitty's sitting-room was perpetually bathed in
a dim, greenish light that filtered through the canopy of
willows, reflecting the lake which almost lapped the old
rosy-pink brick walls at the front of the house. Olive green,
glassy and mysterious, it was sometimes so swollen from
the rains that the tiny island in the middle was completely
under water.

Which long-gone Flowerdew could have had the foolishness to construct a lake in such close proximity to the house?
Sophie had wondered, until she learned that the lake had
come first, being a natural backwater of the river which
flowed along behind the boundaries of the property. The
first Flowerdew had built his house too near the water.
There was a permanent feeling of dampness indoors.
Things left too long in unaired cupboards acquired a patina
of mould, there was often a moist sheen on the flagstones
of the hall, and always this dim, aqueous light in the rooms
facing the lake.

On the eve of Irena's departure Sophie had been there
almost a year. That night Kitty, who was at last beginning

to admit that she was, after all, seventy-seven, was allowing Jessie Crowther to shoo her off to bed without too much protest. She could at times be overbearing and a little auto-cratic, and lately she had lost some of the vitality and sense of fun that had already made Sophie come to love her, that made her seem ageless, despite her disabilities. She'd even been talking about going back to Tunisia, where the climate would be better for her arthritis. Now, bidding them good night, she prepared to go upstairs and drink a last glass of mint tea before bed, leaving the rest of them to their coffee.

'Irena, my dear, we've already said our goodbyes. You'll be gone before I get up in the morning but I wish you well. I wish you very well. Write soon. Good night, everyone, God bless, and sleep well.' As she left the room, Kitty's hand rested affectionately for a moment on Sophie's head; it would have broken the girl's heart to know that this was the last time she would ever see her.

The departure of the two old women left the five of them, as well as Irena herself: Sophie, Madeleine—and Angie Robinson, who always tagged along in Madeleine's wake whenever she could; Felix; and Tommo, having let himself be persuaded to leave his solitary cottage for once to join in the party. If party it could be called, this farewell dinner for Irena.

It was Madeleine who'd suggested to Irena that she was wasted here, that her talents could be used elsewhere, Madeleine who'd brought to her notice the job of translator in a London firm which was expanding its export trade with Germany. It seemed to be a job tailor-made for Irena, whose German was much better than her English, which varied from very good to unintelligible, and who spoke Polish and one or two other Middle European languages as fluently as her native Czech.

But Irena, as was to be expected, had ignored the sugges-tion and went on in her usual noisy, head-on fashion. After all, why should she leave the cushy number she had here?

She had a greedy nature, eager to take what she could get, and at Flowerdew she had a berth for life. Then without warning she announced that she had applied for and been given the position and that she was about to depart the following week. There was an oddly satisfied look about her but she would not explain her change of mind. Kitty likewise refused to add to the speculation that she must at last have had enough, and indicated to Irena that her presence was no longer welcome, though Felix murmured privately to Madeleine that he thought Kitty must have bribed her.

Madeleine's large, short-sighted eyes widened behind her spectacles. She always thought the best of everyone and things like that never appeared to enter her mind.

'Kitty's not exactly poor,' Felix went on. 'And who'd want a daughter like that hanging around the place?'

Madeleine was speechless. She had looked first at Kitty, then Irena. There wasn't a trace of resemblance—was there? Lots of people had lively dark eyes like Irena's, including Irena's father. In any case, she happened to know that Kitty had other plans for her money. She looked across the room to where Kitty was sitting with Sophie, and smiled to herself.

Whatever the reason was for Irena's abrupt turnaround, Kitty, no longer harassed by the threat of violent moods and indigestible cooking, looked as though a weight had been taken from her shoulders, if slightly guilty. But Irena would be all right. Instinctively one knew that. She would always land on her feet. She was a born survivor.

When Kitty and Jessie Crowther had at last gone upstairs, an awkward silence fell languidly upon the rest, a hiatus which none of them had the energy or the will to break through, a lethargy that was partly induced by the heavy meal and the wine to which none of them was accustomed. Even Irena was oddly subdued tonight, as if she regretted the sudden decision to leave what must have been a quiet oasis in her thirty-nine years of nomadic, rootless life. And yet, watching her as she lolled back in her chair, in an ungainly, unaware posture with her knees too far apart, it was impossible to believe her capable of such sentient feelings. Had she been a man, she would have been handsome, the image of her father, Miloslav Bron, who had stood to be photographed with Kitty and Alfred Wilbraham in the desert. As it was, her features were too heavy for a woman. She was swarthy and stocky, with coarse black hair and thick, fiercely black eyebrows, the suspicion of a moustache on her upper lip.

Sophie sank gracefully back into her chair after pouring the coffee, an unconscious but undeniable contrast to Irena. Two pairs of men's eyes followed her. The sexual tension, the vibrations of love and jealousy between the three of them were almost tangible. It was late summer and the windows were open to the soft evening dusk of a sudden and unexpected heatwave: to the lake at the front and the courtyard at the back, where Kitty's white doves cooed softly beyond the low-silled windows, where apricots glowed like golden moons on the espalier trained against the brick wall. The last of the day's heat had brought out the thick scent of damask roses and great waves of fragrance wafted into the room.

Which of them was it who dropped the suggestion into the silence? None of them remembered afterwards. Was it Sophie, dreaming in her pale floating dress, her hair a curtain to her shoulders, aware of young Felix's eyes hungrily on her and Tommo's studiously turning the other way whenever they met hers, who brought the conversation round to the mystery of the future? To where they would all be in ten years' time?

Irena laughed. She had an excited, throaty laugh that was oddly disturbing. 'Such foolishness! To tempt Fate! But if you are really wishink to know, there is a Ouija board in the attic.'

No one asked how she knew this. It was naturally assumed that Irena, with her acquisitive instincts, being what she was and having been at Flowerdew for a year and a half, would have penetrated its secrets from attic to cellar. Despite the cool reception of her suggestion, she went on pressing it and eventually they were all, apart from Tommo, half way persuaded to try. Even Felix, because Sophie wanted it and Tommo did not.

If only they hadn't. If only they'd listened to Tommo's objections.

'Oooh, yes,' cried Angie in the little-girl voice that was irritating beyond endurance, though she usually went against Irena on principle. Her dislike passed over Irena's head; she was impervious to what anyone thought about her, in particular Angie, whom everyone knew was only tolerated by Kitty because of Madeleine: Angie, who was already set into the mould she'd chosen for herself and would keep long after she'd outgrown it—blonde and bouffant of hairstyle, short-statured, mini-skirted. Poor, scarred Angie who was sharp and sly—and much cleverer than she wanted anyone to suspect.

Sophie added her persuasions and in spite of initial misgivings, a subtle excitement began to pervade the room as the idea caught on and lifted the inertia, promising to give some purpose to the rest of the evening. They all looked to Madeleine as final arbiter. Of them all, she was the one most likely to have her feet on the ground and indeed was already looking at her watch and beginning to make signs of leaving. Angie said with a pout, 'But you're not on call this evening, Maddie. There's no need for you to go.'

'All the same, I have to start work early in the morning . . .'

'*And please, not Maddie,*' she would have added to anyone but Angie, hating the diminutive. But Angie could get away with murder as far as Madeleine was concerned and now

Madeleine shrugged good-naturedly and said all right, if that was what they all wanted.

'*Doesn't that girl drive you mad?*' Sophie had once heard Kitty ask her, daring to ask what no one else would, but Madeleine, who was kindness itself, had just smiled. 'Oh, Angie's all right. We understand each other, and I'm used to her.'

Now, in response to her friend's plea, she stayed and it was Tommo who stood up, saying in his abrupt way, 'I'm off. I've no patience with all this. It's childish—and dangerous, what's more. And if you've any sense, Sophie, you'll go home, too.'

Their eyes met and for a long moment held. Sophie wavered; then, contrariwise, smiled. 'Oh, I don't know. What's wrong with a spice of danger?'

Flippancy in her infuriated him, she knew, though he'd only himself to blame. There was a lot of unreadable angst about Tommo which she had tried to understand but, questioning him, gently probing, she had been snubbed. 'You're not mature enough to take your own emotional problems on board, never mind mine,' he'd replied with unthinking cruelty, and though he'd been immediately contrite, neither could forget. He turned away now, and without another word, went out via the window, striding over the low sill. In the ensuing silence, his heavy footsteps could be heard crossing the flagstoned courtyard and presently the latch of the gate was heard to click.

'Well, who's going to get this Ouija board, then?' Sophie asked brightly.

'I will go,' volunteered Irena, lumbering to her feet. 'I am knowink where.'

'Well, go quietly and don't wake Kitty,' Madeleine warned, 'you know how lightly she sleeps—*quietly*, Irena!'

'That woman,' declared Felix as Irena stomped out as noisily as if Madeleine hadn't spoken, 'is not merely irritating, she's impossible.'

'Go easy on her. It is her last night. We owe her that,' Madeleine said. Felix was arrogant and rude, but he was only twenty. All the same, he needed an eye kept on him; you never knew which way he would jump.

'I shall never understand how Kitty sticks her. She's too easily put upon.' Which was rich, coming from Felix, but it had occurred to Sophie, too, although somehow she felt that there was more than Kitty's kind-heartedness involved. There was something about Irena that made her shiver, almost a sense of menace underlying that infuriating smugness. If it wasn't too fanciful one might almost be persuaded to think she had some hold over Kitty.

She was gone some time and when she did arrive back, it was minus the Ouija board. 'Ach, I do not remember where I saw it and is too dark to look now,' she declared, shrugging.

'Well, that's it, then!' Madeleine looked relieved but Sophie, envisaging the rest of the evening which must be got through somehow, was not to be put off.

'We can use a tumbler and the Scrabble counters,' she said, but by the time the tiles had been found and a glass produced Madeleine was again looking at her watch and Felix had lost interest. Angie was half apprehensive, half eager. 'Do you think we should?' She giggled nervously.

'Of course we should!' Sophie was determined not to give up now that they'd gone this far, switching on a lamp and beginning to arrange the letters of the alphabet in a circle round the polished rosewood table.

The dusk had closed in. A small breeze ruffled the water on the lake; drawn by the light, moths and other small insects flew in, recklessly immolating themselves against the lamp. Sophie was suddenly conscious of the adjoining room, with its red walls and its mementoes of ancient Carthage and hideous sacrificial rites. She sometimes thought the room was less of a workroom for Kitty than a shrine to Alfred. Angie hated all mention of it and Sophie herself was often uneasy with it, for less superstitious reasons. She gave a quick glance to see that the door was firmly closed and shivered, wondering for the first time whether they had embarked upon something they didn't understand. But it had gone too far by now; they were all seated round the table, five fingertips already planted upon the base of the upturned glass. Angie was excited, her other hand fiddling with her hair, drawing the flick-up at the side further across the livid mark on her face, Madeleine was endeavouring not to look embarrassed at having condoned this, Felix still had that superciliously amused expression imprinted on his face; his pale, cold eyes looked glassy, almost colourless. He'd definitely had too much to drink —but perhaps they all had. Especially Irena.

Her eyes, too, glittered, and the excitement had brought a flush to her swarthy cheeks. Wearing the barbaric jewellery Kitty had given her as a farewell gift, she looked more foreign to Sophie than ever. Of them all, she was the only one who was not either amused, embarrassed or half-scared, though none of them quite knew how to start.

After a small silence Felix began by asking in a facetious, sepulchral tone if anyone was there.

'You should not laugh!' Irena reprimanded him sharply. 'Ask if there is message for anyone, Sophie.'

Sophie cleared her throat and asked the question self-consciously. The glass began to move: I-R-E-N-A.

'That was predictable!'

Felix's laugh was unkind, but this time Irena ignored him and spoke excitedly. 'Who is there?'

D-I-D- The glass stopped. Irena's gasp caught in her throat.

'Do you have message for us?'

E-L-I-S- . . .

At that point the glass skidded madly and slid away, knocking several letters off the table. The nervous silence was fractured by Angie's frightened gasp, followed by

Irena's guttural, accusing voice: 'Elissa! She is wishink to spell Dido, then Elissa, but you, Felix, you push the glass!'

Felix uttered a word not likely to be in Irena's vocabulary, but she got the gist.

'Is not a joke!' she shouted, turning on him. Her pronunciation and command of English was rapidly deteriorating into the accents of farce but Sophie saw that she was deadly earnest. 'And you frighten Angie!'

'I—I'm not scared,' Angie denied, white and trembling by now. Any reference to Carthage and the darker elements of its past was likely to upset her. Kitty, telling her ghoulish stories with relish, had brought the past too vividly into the present and Angie, who was impressionable, hated them; detested Kitty's workroom, the red walls, the blue and red and gold mask of Tanit above the desk, and all the other reminders of fire and magic and evil, however long ago they had occurred. Felix knew this and it was quite possible he had mischievously pushed the glass in order to frighten her, but really it was Irena who was his target tonight. He began bickering with her again.

'Oh, for heaven's sake, do be quiet, you'll wake the old ladies!' Madeleine ordered, even her patience wearing thin. It was unlikely that Jessie Crowther would be disturbed; she was growing deaf and in any case slept like a log, but if Kitty was awakened from her first sleep, she vowed that she never slept a wink for the rest of the night.

'It must be our collective subconscious,' Sophie put in, trying to harmonize the situation. 'When we see the obvious beginning to a word, we all start willing it to move to the next letter—'

'Collective balls!' Felix gave a bark of unamused laughter. 'One of us *must* have been pushing the glass—but it wasn't me. Tommo was right. I've had enough of this voodoo!'

Sophie, too, by now, felt that enough was enough, and as everyone else began to voice their own opinion, the noise level increased. Somewhere above, a floorboard creaked.

'I told you you'd waken Kitty!' Madeleine accused.

'Well then, go up and see if she wants to join in. She can take my place and welcome,' Felix answered flippantly.

'We start again!' Irena announced with authority. 'Come, sit!' She began to rearrange the tiles. 'Is only a game.'

Did any of them believe this by now? However, with varying degrees of unwillingness, they were all, even Angie, eventually persuaded to begin once more and after one or two initial skirmishes, the glass again moved. And now it spelled K-I-T-T-Y. 'You see!' Sophie said, 'Madeleine mentioned Kitty's name and now look—'

'Sssh!' hissed Irena.

The glass had begun to move again. D-E-A-T- it spelled. Before the word was finished, it skidded and stopped.

'Oooh!' Angie wailed, white-faced, her eyes enormous and dangerously bright.

'You do it again, Felix!' Irena was in a fury, but Felix's amusement had now vanished totally. He was no longer prepared to laugh, or even make sarcastic comments. He was as angry as she was, his face ugly with temper. He jumped up, pushing himself from the table with his hands and in doing so, rocked it so that the glass slid off the polished surface, followed by a slither of letters, and splintered on to the floor in a thousand shards of light.

Irena was beside herself. Screaming, she launched herself towards Felix like a wild cat. Sophie, perhaps with some premonition of a horror she could never have envisaged, tried to ward her off, appalled at the way they were acting, like barbarians, at how easily the fragile calm of the hour before had been shattered. Angie began to cry, adding to the hubbub, while Madeleine endeavoured without success to calm everyone down. Footsteps were heard outside: Tommo returning, no doubt ashamed of his boorish departure, perhaps remembering he'd left without even a civil word of farewell to Irena.

Felix, with an exclamation of distaste, suddenly brushed Irena off as if she were some sort of disgusting fly and with great strides left the room. Unstoppable, she flew after him. Their voices could still be heard when they reached the hall, loud but indistinguishable. In the room above, footsteps shuffled across the floor, a door banged. A moment or two later, there was a crash, and after that there was silence. A silence that went on and on.

'Stay here, you two,' Madeleine ordered, walking to the door. Sophie had no desire to do anything else and stayed rooted to the spot but Angie crept after her. Sophie waited alone, trembling, until the waiting became intolerable and then she, too, went into the hall.

CHAPTER 6

A couple of hours' sleep after getting the murder inquiry under way wasn't much, but after breakfast, a sharp shower and a change of clothes you were good for another twelve hours. No wonder, though, that Howard Cherry had opted for promotion that bound him more and more to the desk but at least promised a fair share of good night's sleep! But Mayo didn't really envy the Super. Cherry was a good friend and welcome to his promotion. It was where he'd been aiming ever since he and Mayo had been young coppers together, working on the same beat in the north of England. Mayo was a practical policeman while Cherry was a born administrator who was willing to rely on Mayo to get on with the job so long as he was kept well in the picture, a situation which suited both of them very well.

After performing this function as soon as he got to the station, Mayo came down from the third floor to find

Kite returned from Pennybridge, waiting for him with the
name of someone who could put him in touch with the
relatives of the murdered woman so that they could get
a positive identification. Her name, he said, was Freeman,
Dr Madeleine Freeman.

Kite didn't look as though his own sleep had done him
much good; there were pouches under his eyes, but he was
full of nervous energy, unable to keep still, and it soon
became evident why. He was jubilant with the news that
one of his informers had contacted him with a possible lead
on the whereabouts of the disappearing witness in the child
pornography case. It would mean, he remarked, a drive
down to Essex for someone that morning, would mean
taking two off the strength just when manpower was needed
most. It was a statement made partly in query, partly in
hope.

'Better get off then, hadn't you, Martin? It's your case
and we're not letting them slip through the net at this
stage.'

Mayo would be glad to see the end of it himself, for more
reasons than one. It had been an emotionally slanted affair
and a successful outcome would give a fillip to every man
and woman on the strength.

Kite could hardly conceal his satisfaction at the hoped-
for-reply, but he tried. 'Couldn't have come at a worse time,
I know, but we can't let up until we've got these bastards.'

Mayo hoped Kite wasn't letting this one get to him. His
normal, cheerful insouciance had been remarkable for its
absence since he'd been dealing with this admittedly depressing inquiry. It was understandable—he had two boys
of his own and an investigation of this sort was the pits,
but Kite was a police officer and the rotten, mucky things
of life were his business—he'd better snap out of it if he
thought otherwise. You couldn't afford to become involved
to the point where your efficiency and sense of judgement

were impaired. And yet, without it, without the pity and the rage, what was the point?

'Keep at it, Martin,' he said.

All available manpower would now be called upon for the murder investigation, but the possibility of letting up on the case which had occupied the time and skills of the department for so long was a non-starter. Mayo was used to handling half a dozen cases at once, as they all were. It was simply a question of who now did what, how much routine work he himself could delegate to his inspector, the mature and unflappable Atkins. He mentally surveyed the rest of his team, most of whose strengths and weaknesses he could gauge to a millimetre.

'Sergeant Moon,' he said, 'I'll keep Abigail Moon with me for the most part of this one and leave you free to concentrate on Billen. You take Farrar with you today.'

He wasn't displeased with this strategy. He felt it to be an adroit compensating move on his part, killing two birds with one stone, one that would give Abigail the experience she needed—without rubbing Farrar's nose in it. Of all the team, he was the one who resented the woman detective's presence most, as being about to achieve (without much effort, as he saw it) the promotion which continually escaped him. He wouldn't see why, for instance, he, rather than Abigail Moon, should have been sent with Kite, but tough. That's the way we all had it once, lad.

Abigail, unlike Farrar, was delighted.

Her plans for her future were not going too badly. If only she had as much confidence in her personal life as in her professional one! Although her academic prowess at university hadn't been particularly brilliant, she'd obtained a respectable degree and she knew, backed up by the assessments she'd undergone so far, that she was capable, given the opportunities and a share of luck, of rising to a senior position in the force. She had no illusions about what she'd be up against. Even if it was an exaggeration to say that she'd have to be twice as good as any of her male colleagues to get anywhere, the way ahead was certain to be tough, and since this present case was going to give her the opportunity to get her foot in the door, she was determined she wasn't going to miss a trick. She was going to enjoy the new experience of a murder hunt, of working with the team. No one could be easier to get on with than Martin Kite and she could ignore Farrar, whom she liked well enough when he wasn't acting like a jealous prima donna. The rest of the team were friendly and she thought she would like the challenge of working for Mayo, despite his reputation for being a bloody-minded Yorkshireman when the occasion demanded it, and a slave-driver to boot. She didn't mind either; she could cope with the one and rather admired the other—especially since she'd found he worked twice as hard himself. She'd also heard he was a right old male chauvinist—but then, ninety per cent of her colleagues were.

She rang Madeleine Freeman's home as soon as she could after their return from Pennybridge, but all she got was the answering service, advising her to try the surgery. There, she received a frosty reception from the dragon who answered, to the effect that Doctor couldn't *possibly* see anyone that morning, it wasn't her scheduled surgery. In the end, a reluctant concession was achieved, as it finally got through that this was urgent police business: they could come in about nine-thirty and catch Doctor between house-visits. That was when she usually popped in to the surgery to see if any more calls had come in for her and to pick up her post.

The tiny patch of flowerbed through which a few sparrow-bitten crocuses had mistakenly pushed hopeful heads didn't make the brick-built surgery look any less like a British Telecom sub-station. A small, dumpy erection, it squatted on the edge of the Somerville estate in the middle of an area of waste ground which was advertised as being ripe for development. According to the board outside, the all-woman partnership was shared with Dr Aisha Lall and Dr Mary Smith; inside, the patients jammed into the small waiting-room were mostly harassed-looking women and noisy, under-schoolage children with runny noses and hacking coughs.

'Another five minutes and you'd have missed her! Doctor's just about to set off again, but she'll see you for a few minutes,' the dragon announced, brisk and condescending, intimating that this was an unheard-of favour. Middle-aged, grey and officious, she held the telephone between her chin and her shoulder while walking the fingers of one hand through patient-record envelopes in the filing cabinet, and at the same time dealing with a patient on the end of the line. 'Right, Mrs Painter, I've given you eleven, OK? Don't be late or you'll miss your appointment.' Replacing the receiver smartly, she tapped figures into a small computer by her side, and only then did she jerk her head towards a door in the corner marked: PLEASE KNOCK AND ENTER. 'In there,' she ordered the two detectives. 'Don't forget to knock before you go in.'

'No, ma'am,' Mayo said.

Dr Freeman already had her coat on and was finishing a mug of coffee while writing something on a prescription pad. Mayo was beginning to feel a serious lack of initiative in himself at having only one object in view. She motioned them to sit down but remained standing while she asked what she could do for them.

Abigail told her who they were and that they were investigating the suspicious death of a woman. 'We're hoping you may be able to help in identifying her.'

'Oh dear! Yes, of course I'll help if you think I can— one of my patients, was she?' The doctor looked grave, but not unduly disturbed. Death, after all, came within the

daily scope of her job. Pushing her papers away, she
regarded them inquiringly, giving her mind immediately to
what was being said, a tall, collected sort of woman with
steady eyes behind large spectacles, a firm, smiling mouth,
a well-cut hairstyle, large calm doctor's hands with short,
unvarnished nails. Her skin was glowing and entirely without make-up. She looked as wholesome as new bread and
eminently sensible.

'We think her name might be Angie Robinson.'

Death took on a different aspect when it was someone
you knew. However familiar it was to her, professionally
speaking, however accustomed she was to helping patients
cope, it didn't help the doctor now. She sat down abruptly
but after an interval of absolute stillness, and though her
face had drained of colour, she braced herself, sat upright
and asked without a tremor, 'What makes you think it's
her?'

'One of my men thought he recognized her,' Mayo said.
'She has a very distinctive birthmark . . .'

It was evidently the answer she'd feared. 'Yes, I see. I
see.'

'We shall need a formal identification of course. Her next
of kin . . . ?'

'She has none.' The doctor took a deep breath. 'I'm prepared to identify her.'

'It won't be pleasant, I'm afraid.' He told her how Angie
Robinson—if it was her—had died, and where.

'Better me than anyone else. It won't be the first time
I've seen a dead body. And I was closer to her than anyone.'

'Perhaps we should see a photograph first, if you have
one.' He was reluctant to subject her to an ordeal which
might, despite the near certainty, be unnecessary. But it
was immediately obvious, when she produced a snapshot
from her handbag, that the woman pictured there, and the
one now lying on the mortuary slab, were one and the same

person. Even though the profile turned to the camera had been her unmarked side.

Yes, that was Angie Robinson, the doctor agreed ten minutes later, looking down with a frozen expression at her friend, decently covered apart from the face, laid out in the County Hospital mortuary chapel. She was silent for a long time, but before turning away she stretched out a hand towards the body and gently, almost caressingly, pulled forward the hair so that it more or less covered the livid mark on the face. 'Poor love, she minded so terribly anyone seeing it.'

When they were again outside Mayo reminded her that it would be necessary to talk. 'Is there somewhere here in the hospital where we can have a few minutes?'

The doctors' common room was her first suggestion, but on second thoughts it would be better, she amended swiftly, if they went across to where she lived in Kilbracken Road, only a few streets away. It was the only way to be certain there'd be no interruptions. Mayo glanced at his watch, saw there was time since the PM wasn't scheduled to take place for another hour, and agreed. Their car followed her Volvo along the circuitous ring road to a quiet, tree-lined road situated between the hospital and the red brick buildings of Lavenstock College. Parking outside a sizeable terrace house with a house agent's sign planted in the garden, she ran quickly up the steps and unlocked the door.

The room she took them into was spacious and high-ceilinged with wide, sashed windows, a fireplace with a mahogany surround and mirrored overmantel, and a general air of solid, unimaginative comfort, apparently furnished in the early years of the century and largely untouched since. The heavy, drab-coloured curtains and Persian-patterned carpet muffled the sounds from outside as she bent to switch on an electric fire in the grate. 'Tell me about it, please. I'd like to know the details, though it's

going to take time to absorb. Hartopp Moor! Why on earth
should she be out there—and why, *why* should anyone want
to kill Angie anyway?'

It was the question they all asked, understandably, mani-
festing the normal person's bewilderment when faced with
the incomprehension of violent death. '*Why her, or him?*' And
usually, '*What have they ever done to deserve this?*' though quite
often the answer to that one was patently obvious. Mayo
never attempted to answer the unanswerable, and in this
case she didn't seem to expect it. He said, 'I have to ask
you if she'd quarrelled with anyone lately, or if there was
someone likely to have had a grudge against her?'

'Nobody. I would have known if there had been.'

'When was the last time you saw her?'

'On Sunday. She had lunch with me.'

'How was she? Did she seem any different from usual?'

'No, just the same Angie I've always known.'

He said, 'Did she have any particular man friend?'

The doctor blinked, then shook her head decisively.
Angie had known very few men. To be truthful, she hadn't
had a very high opinion of the opposite sex. 'She had a
rotten childhood, her father was a man with an evil temper,
a beast of a man who used to beat both her and her mother,
and eventually left them when Angie was thirteen.' She
gave a twisted smile. 'As you might imagine, it made her
very choosy who she went out with. And also, she was very
conscious of her face . . . though she needn't have been. It
wasn't so very bad, and when you knew her you forgot
about the mark.'

All at once, tears sprang to her eyes, seeming to startle
her as much as her audience. 'Excuse me,' she mumbled,
taking off her spectacles and fumbling for her handkerchief
to rub them angrily away, as if ashamed of them. 'Please
excuse me.'

Without asking, Abigail crossed to a drinks tray set out
on a side table, poured and brought back a long glass of

mineral water. 'Thank you.' The doctor drank thirstily. 'You must forgive me, it's been such a shock.' Clutching the half-full glass as if it were a comfort to hold on to something stable, she said, 'We'd known each other since we were at school together and I've always felt myself responsible for her—she was never really very good at looking after herself.'

A nice woman but very earnest, the doctor, Mayo summed her up, the sort of woman who felt it incumbent upon her to be responsible for others.

'As a matter of fact,' she went on, 'she lived here with me until recently—until she moved out and got another place. Perhaps if she hadn't . . .'

'I noticed your house is up for sale. Is that why she did that?'

'Did what?'

'Moved out.'

'Oh. Oh yes. I'm getting married next month, and moving out as soon as possible.'

'Congratulations. Who's the lucky man?'

'His name's Bouvier, Edward Bouvier, he's a vascular surgeon. A little late in the day for both of us, but . . .' She rubbed at the frown line between her brows, as if she had a headache, but a little of her lost colour returned to her face.

Mayo was mildly surprised. Madeleine Freeman was undoubtedly an attractive woman, in her late thirties, he guessed, not an unusually late age for marriage, considering the times. Women—he was well aware of this, to his cost —now wanted to make sure of their careers before committing themselves to marriage and family life. But she had immediately struck him as a woman who would value her independence too much for that. That her caring would be at a distance; a woman essentially central to herself.

'We've bought a new house at Tannersley, a modern

house. New furniture, much more to my taste than all this,' she said, her quick glance sweeping round the room, accompanied by a slight shiver, as if dismissive of old ghosts and echoes. 'All this will go.'

'Quite a change in your life, then,' Mayo remarked. 'And in Miss Robinson's, too, I imagine?'

Quickly, she said, 'Yes, but she was very happy for me. In any case, we never expected to live together permanently. We always knew it was possible that one of us might want to move out for some reason, or get married . . .' She hesitated. 'She had the chance of a very nice flat in Bulstrode Street a few weeks ago and decided to move in immediately. She didn't want to be left here on her own for any length of time.'

Mayo knew Bulstrode Street but kept his expression neutral. After this? Bulstrode Street? Right in the middle of the sad no man's land of bedsits and one-person flats just beyond the town centre. An enclave for single people, living alone, many of them women—and as such, an area with an ongoing prowler problem. Abigail caught his eye. Maybe, their exchange of glances said, they'd have the answer to her death sooner than they imagined.

Maybe, thought Mayo, adding to himself that the dead woman was unlikely to have been as happy at the change in her fortunes as the good doctor wanted to think. Her naïve assumption of her friend's acceptance of the big change in her life surely involved a certain amount of self-deception, or even guilt, that she herself was coming off decidedly better in the switch-round than Angie. He reminded himself of the photo of the murdered woman, now in his pocket. Petite, with a lot of blonde hair, an above-the-knees skirt, wearing the high heels that many short women considered indispensable. But that first assumption, at the first sight of her body with its disarranged clothes, that she'd been a tart, that was all wrong

—he'd been right to have doubts about that. One look at the closed, prim little face told you otherwise. She was simply the sort of woman, he suspected, who had got herself locked into a style of dressing that had once suited her, with a hairstyle that was many years too young for her ageing face and a skirt length, despite its current fashion, several inches too short for her. A woman, he strongly suspected, afraid of growing old.

'I shouldn't have let her go,' Dr Freeman said abruptly. 'I should have looked after her better. But it was only temporary, that flat of hers, until she got herself fixed up with somewhere better. Though as a matter of fact, I'm inclined to think she'd probably already found it. At lunch on Sunday she was very excited. She'd only hint at what it was but I guessed. She was like that, you know—she used to get a childish enjoyment out of keeping a secret, she liked to keep you guessing.' The ghost of a smile briefly touched the corners of her lips. 'She spoke about a very important meeting with some man and she laughed and said it was going to change her future, and in the context of what we'd been speaking about, I took it to mean she was going to view some new accommodation.' Her long capable fingers convulsively clutched the glass that had held the mineral water. 'Oh God, perhaps I was wrong—'

'No, that may be very helpful. We'll make inquiries with all the house agents in the town, unless . . . This man—I don't suppose she told you his name, where he lived, what he did for a living?'

'Nothing at all. Though I must confess I wasn't paying all that much attention. I had other things on my mind, the new house for one thing . . .'

He finally stood up, after establishing that the doctor had had a surgery the previous day until seven. She'd gone straight home when it finished and at eight-fifteen her fiancé, Edward Bouvier, had called to take her to dine out.

He wasn't entirely satisfied with the interview. Abigail

had taken several pages of notes—but even so, what they had about the dead woman didn't amount to much more than an eyeful of cold tea. She had worked at the Women's Hospital as a clerk on the reception desk. Angela Margaret Robinson, aged 38, unmarried, unattached. No special friends other than Dr Freeman, no interests except helping tirelessly in the doctor's campaign to keep the Women's Hospital open. It didn't sound much of a life, nor give any indication of the sort of woman she had been, popular or disliked, happy or dissatisfied. She must have had her hopes and aspirations, too, but this bald outline revealed nothing except that she had seemingly been content to live in the shadow of her friend. There was nothing on this showing that could have led to someone wanting to murder her.

'What was she really like?' he asked in a final attempt to fill out the picture. 'It always helps to know what sort of person—'

'I'm sorry, that really is more than I feel able to cope with just yet. You'll have to give me time. Later, perhaps . . .'

'I understand.'

Her distress was evident, perhaps through fear of letting emotion get the better of her again, and Mayo felt that any more questioning was likely to be counter-productive. They were only ferreting around at this stage for anything they could pick up that might be of use. More relevant questions could come later, if necessary.

She took leave of them at the door, already shrugging on her coat again and exclaiming at the time, 'I must get on!'

'You've had a shock,' Mayo said. 'Couldn't you get one of your partners to take your calls today?'

'Good heavens, that won't be necessary, I'm far too busy!' She added wanly, 'And mooning around being miserable isn't likely to bring Angie back to life, is it?'

'Well, take my advice, and don't overdo it.'

In his sympathy for her, he'd forgotten he was talking to

a doctor and she managed a smile. 'And if you'll take *my* advice, you'll go home and get a few hours' sleep, yourself. You look as though you could do with it.'

CHAPTER 7

The house had come alive again now that Sophie was home. All the rooms were in use again, not merely the kitchen. Fresh flowers filled the vases, the elusive scent she used lingered everywhere. (Maggie had heard she had the scent specially made for her in Paris—or perhaps it was New York—and had no difficulty in believing it.) She ordered delicious and expensive food, nibbling at minute portions and leaving the rest for Maggie, for Sophie ate less than a mouse.

Maggie wasn't grumbling. Her student days weren't long behind; she was always short of money, and lobster and fillet steak were a decided improvement on baked beans and beefburgers.

'I suppose you want me to pack up and go, now that I've finished my house-sitting stint,' she said.

'Now, darling, don't be tiresome. You know you can stay as long as you want. Anyway, I don't think I shall be here all that long. It's always so cold in England.'

'The thermostat's up to eighty! I don't know how you can stand it!'

'Well, hie thee off to an attic, it's cold enough up there, and get on with your painting. I've held you up long enough this morning.'

'True,' said Maggie, with a laugh, disappearing in a gust of energy to immerse herself in one of the large and violent abstracts which Sophie could never understand, while she herself, thin and elegant in her dress of fine soft wool, the colour of aubergines, drew her chair up to the desk near the fire to read her post, shivering in an exaggerated manner at imaginary draughts. But she loved England more every time she returned to it, realizing how much she missed this house where she'd been born. It was a small Queen Anne gem of a house on what had once been the village green at Pennybridge, its light, square rooms perfectly proportioned, the pale honey-coloured walls setting off her collection of gold-framed Baxter prints, the gathering together of which had become something of an obsession over the years.

Perhaps this time she'd stay. Perhaps it was time to stop running away. Sometimes recently she'd found herself in some part of Europe or America with no memory of why she'd decided on that particular place, and little idea of how she'd ever got there. She'd achieved the freedom she had so longed for at eighteen, and found by bitter experience that this meant she couldn't bear to tie herself down to anyone or anything. Now there was nothing and no one who really mattered—unless it was Roz, and young Michael. And also, perhaps . . . But deliberately, and now by habit, she switched her mind away from subjects that were unremittingly painful.

'Do you still write?' Felix had asked her last night, sitting opposite her in the firelit room, under the golden light of the lamps, while she sat curled up on the pale Chinese carpet, her legs folded beneath her, her hands held out to the glowing coals. They were simulated coals but they gave an illusion of warmth and the gas flames were real enough.

After a long time she'd said no.

'Why not, Sophie? You had such hopes—'

'We all did. We were young, we believed ourselves capable of anything.'

'*But you were never a real writer,*' Tommo had said the last time she saw him, '*and never will be.*' His outspokenness, not having softened with the years, had initially enraged her but, thinking about it later, she had been forced to acknowledge that he might well be right, though it was painful to accept: she didn't have the passion, the determination to slog on that Maggie had, for instance, young as she was. Yet she had found compensations, other things she could do: she had discovered in herself an unexpected acuity in financial matters so that now she managed not only her own affairs but, ironically, Roz's as well.

Felix hadn't pressed the point. 'I went to Flowerdew before I came here,' he said abruptly, shocking her, though it was a logical enough follow-on from his previous remarks.

'What? You didn't!' Sophie knew that her eyes were startled, frightened, as she raised them to meet his unblinking stare.

'It was a mistake'.

She had caught the echoes of fear in her own voice and controlled it as best she could as she answered lightly, 'Well, it always is a mistake to go back, they say, don't they?' In his case, she would have thought, an act of unprecedented folly. Her heart had begun to bang. Horrified at what his return might mean, she tried to change the subject, to ask him about his present life, his marriage, his work, but he interrupted her.

'Don't you ever think about Flowerdew, and Kitty—about what happened, Sophie?'

'No!'

'Doesn't it ever weigh on your conscience?'

'I don't let it,' she said evenly.

'Are you sure?'

'Of course I'm sure! I don't see any reason for tormenting myself with something that's over and done with. We swore we would forget it.' And she had, with that strength of purpose she could always summon when she needed it. She had locked it away in a dark cupboard at the back of her mind and told herself that she had thrown the key away. It was the only way she could have coped. 'I don't want to talk about it.'

'But I do. We must.'

'Felix—' she began.

'No, you have to listen.'

The words fell like sharp marble chips, his eyes were that icy pale blue they always used to be when he was angry.

Fourteen years ago he had imagined himself in love with her and had tried to persuade her that she was in love with him. It would have been easy enough to go along with that—he'd been very attractive in a confident, self-aware fashion, as intent on finding an identity for himself as she had been, though quite differently. His hadn't then been the successful, smart image he projected now, but he was working on it even then—short hair, high collars and tailored suits when everyone else of his generation was long-haired and wearing jeans and T-shirts; the affectation of writing his forename with an acute accent, his surname with an apostrophe between the D and the a, pretending he had French ancestry. Félix D'Arbell. Like Tess Durbeyfield, Miss D'Urberville. Perhaps he still wrote it that way.

But, quite apart from the ever-present fact of Tommo that had begun to dominate her life, she'd never liked the ambition that drove him, the ruthlessness that he would certainly need to get to the top. She had always felt alarmed by his temper, which could explode into a sudden rage. She knew now that she'd been right not to let him persuade her, even though the years had changed him somewhat. He was more in control, less inclined to let his feelings get the better of him. All the same, she would never make the mistake of underestimating him.

'Have you contacted the others?' she asked.

'No.'

'Why me?' He didn't answer. 'Why have you really come back, Felix, after all this time?'

'Don't you know? Are you really telling me you don't know?'

And Sophie, to her chagrin, found herself trembling and quite unable to meet his cold, challenging stare.

CHAPTER 8

Angie Robinson had been only one of the growing number of women in Lavenstock who for one reason or another lived alone. Many of them had drifted like shifting sand into the district around the bypass, where affordable accommodation was still to be found—affordable largely on account of its being so run down. The noise, Mayo supposed, must have made its own contribution; rarely was it quiet, day or night. Cars, lorries and buses ground along, stopped and started at the traffic lights, changed gear and gunned engines ceaselessly. Run down and noisy, with two rows of identical houses facing each other, on-street parking jamming it from end to end, Bulstrode Street escaped neither condition.

Atkins had already started the process of rounding up the pathetic bunch of known prowlers, Peeping Toms, sexual deviants of all kinds who were known to frequent the area —twenty-eight to date, and more to come—and though there was always the chance that one of them might prove to be the killer, Mayo was increasingly less hopeful that this would be the case. They were a sorry lot. Some had access to a car in which the body might have been transported away from the scene of the crime, others probably had the nous to think of taking it away. Not many had both.

Having decided there was time for a quick look round Angie Robinson's flat before the PM, Mayo, accompanied by Abigail Moon, let himself in with the key Angie had given Madeleine Freeman for emergencies. The flat proved to be an upstairs one, really only the bedroom floor of the house, having its own access by means of a door at the bottom of a flight of exceedingly narrow stairs. The whole place had evidently been recently redecorated and the smell of paint still lingered. Dead white paint, no doubt in an effort to lighten the gloom, but the effect was about as welcoming as a cold bath on a winter morning, an icy white contained silence in contrast with the distant grinding traffic noise outside.

'Not exactly home from home, is it?'

Mayo stood in the front room with his hands in his pockets, getting the feel of the place, not knowing what it was about this particular flat that should make him take such an instant and intense dislike to it . . . he'd seen many far, far worse. It was clean and more than adequate for one person: really nothing to take exception to . . . except there was no warmth, it possessed not even a modicum of individuality, the general clutter of well-loved possessions that characterizes almost every human life.

The sitting-room contained nothing but a couple of easy chairs and a laminated coffee table still smelling of its factory finish, dumped in the middle of a dreary beige carpet. A packing case or two was pushed against the walls, and that was it. Not even a few bookshelves, houseplants or a television set: but in the centre of the coffee table was a half-full whisky bottle and a used glass. Poor Angie Robinson. So this was where she'd arrived. Drinking alone in this chilling apartment.

'Looks as though she was only just getting round to the finishing touches,' Abigail remarked, but he saw his own feelings mirrored in the tiny shiver of distaste. 'Not making much headway, was she, to say she's been here six weeks?'

This was patently true. The packing cases had been opened but not yet emptied. Lifting their lids, a pile of cushions was revealed stuffed into one, and another appeared to be full of ornaments and knick-knacks. Several pictures leant against the wall. A chain-store print of a striped tiger had already been hung, but the X-hooks, hammer, picture cord and scissors for fixing the rest had been abandoned on the floor beneath it.

First appearances didn't suggest that any sort of struggle had taken place here. If there were any hidden traces, any tell-tale signs of anyone else's presence, they wouldn't remain hidden for long, for Dexter and his SOCO team were due to move in and it was Dexter's unshakable theory that nobody could kill without leaving some telltale signs and that he could, moreover, find an eyelash in a sand-storm. Before the team arrived to do the necessary detailed work, however, a preliminary look around was indicated.

'Let's get started.' Mayo decided to begin with the kitchen and bathroom, leaving the bedroom to Abigail. 'You know what to look for—basically, anything that strikes you.'

At least Angie had tried to make the bedroom more wel-coming. Although it, too, was painted in the same unin-spired white as the rest of the flat, there were some flowery, pastel peach curtains, with duvet cover and pillow-cases to match, which did have some sort of softening effect.

Abigail began with the dressing-table, hands encased in thin plastic gloves, doing her best not to make value judge-ments—but wow! the woman hadn't stinted herself, had she? She blinked, viewing the array of high-priced bottles and jars of cosmetics, lotions, powders and scents spread over the polished surface. How could anyone bring them-selves to spend that much on make-up? Then, catching a glimpse of herself in the mirror, her shining bronze plait and a clear, glowing skin that owed little to artifice, she felt suddenly less inclined to criticize, recalling that livid birthmark Angie Robinson had gone through life bearing on her face. But she couldn't stop her eyebrows rising even further when she opened the drawers and saw the piles of seductive underwear, the slips and briefs in pure silk, the satin cami-knickers, the lacy bras. Hm. And the wardrobe, crammed with attention-grabbing clothes that all the same didn't come cheap. And more shoes than Imelda Marcos, all of them frivolous and impractical.

Abigail might not admire Angie's taste but she couldn't fault the care she'd taken of her things. Clothes on hangers. Shoes on trees. No drawers full of laddered tights, no dirty underwear hanging around, no gooey make-up jars. But the clutter in the brown leather shoulder-bag which she picked up off the bed was like everyone else's. She tipped the whole lot out on to the bed: keys, wallet, coin-purse and diary, a couple of used tissues, several one pence pieces, till receipts and screwed-up shopping-lists. Straightening out one of these, she stared at it with mounting excitement, then went to find Mayo.

He had come across nothing of special interest in the bathroom. In the kitchen only some leftover chicken and salad in the fridge, a few tins in the cupboards, the empty foil carton of a frozen, calorie-controlled dinner-for-one (vegetable lasagne) in the waste-bin.

Abigail came out of the bedroom, holding out by the corner a brown envelope for his inspection. 'I think you should take a look at this, sir.' She couldn't hide the quick excitement in her voice.

Creased and folded over, the envelope had several items of shopping written on the back. Mayo had only seen that particular handwriting once before but there was no mistaking it. He realized why Abigail looked so animated.

'Any writing materials in the bedroom?' he asked after running his eyes quickly down the list. Abigail shook her head. 'We'd better try in here then, it's the only place left,' he said, looking round the sitting-room, 'but where? At the bottom of one of those damn great packing cases, I'll bet.' But very soon, at the back of the only drawer there was, the one in the coffee table, they found what they were looking for: a box of writing paper, shaded from pale pink to deepest rose.

Mayo tried to remember the contents of a month-old letter he'd read only briefly at the time, to sort the facts out in his mind, while Abigail put in carefully, feeling a sense of vindication but wondering how far her opinions would be welcomed at this point, 'The letter's making a bit more sense now, isn't it?'

'Is it?' Mayo growled absently. 'Tell me how.'

'Angie Robinson must have known the old woman archæologist Sophie Lawrence worked for . . . Roz Spalding said that was how Sophie had met Angie, after all. So all that business of Dido-Elissa, and Tanit, and the cremation urns and whatnot falls into place, if she—the old woman—worked on the ruins at Carthage, I mean—'

'—and if we're talking about murder, and she was the victim?'

'It does look as though she might have been, doesn't it, sir?' Abigail persisted doggedly. 'And if Angie knew this, that provides a motive for *her* murder . . . you remember what she wrote, that she'd been quiet for too long . . .' She fell silent. The clear ideas in her mind didn't sound nearly so logical when she spoke them aloud.

Mayo smiled suddenly, quickly recovering from the speed with which she'd overtaken him, zipping by in the fast lane while he'd been stooging along in the centre. He was going to have to watch it, working with her. Which might, he acknowledged, be no bad thing. Occasionally. 'Good thinking, Abigail. It's worth trying on the dog, anyway,' he admitted, with one of his rare smiles. 'Any ideas are welcome at this stage. Blackmail being the first that springs to mind.'

Which was, in fact, the strongest possibility . . . now that it was known that Angie had been the letter-writer. Or now that it was ninety-nine per cent certain she'd written it. It was coming back to him: '*I've kept quiet for fourteen years and said nothing. But I was wrong. Murder should be punished.*' So she'd felt she couldn't keep quiet any longer? And had been silenced before she could speak?

'It's possible,' he said.

Especially if Angie's bank account revealed a sudden influx of money. If her bank book had been found. But it hadn't, nor had any other of her private papers. 'They may be in one of the packing cases,' he said, 'but we'll leave those until the SOCO boys have finished. Or there may be things still left at Kilbracken Road. See that her room there's checked, will you?'

'Right, sir.'

'Which means there are two things missing, so far—her papers and her other earring.' The latter being a piece of jewellery of some size which one or other of them would surely have spotted if she had been murdered here and it had been lost in the struggle.

Abigail said, 'She had a current account with Lloyds. Her cheque-book was in her handbag.'

'Right. Make me an appointment to see her bank manager, will you? Better still, let me talk to him.'

'I'll do it now.' She went immediately to the telephone and a moment later was speaking to the bank. 'All right, I'll tell him.' She put a hand over the receiver. 'The manager's away for a couple of days. You can talk to the assistant manager, though.'

'Tell them I'll wait.' Pushed as he was, Mayo couldn't see the harm in waiting a couple of days to see the manager, a man whom he knew, rather than his assistant, who might not be so forthcoming. When Abigail had rung off, he said, 'Meanwhile, I think we should talk to the people she worked with . . . get some idea what she was like, what sort of life she led—and check with these other people concerned in this hospital campaign—they may be able to throw some light on her movements last night. And I suppose we'd better see Sophie Lawrence. At least we shall find out from her who this old woman is—or was.'

Before leaving the house, Mayo pressed the bell of the downstairs flat over the name I. Kitchener, waited, then pressed again. A curtain had been twitched, there had been sounds through the door of a radio or television turned to maximum when they'd arrived and although all was now silent, it was odds on someone was inside there, listening. Eventually shuffling footsteps were heard, the door was opened on the chain and one faded blue eye looked out.

'Who is it?'

'Police.'

'What?'

Abigail pushed her warrant card through the opening. After a moment it was handed back and the door opened by an old woman who was breathing asthmatically and leaning heavily on a zimmer frame, a little flustered but regarding them expectantly.

'Come in,' she wheezed, 'come in! Sorry about the chain, and keeping you waiting. Takes me some time to get on my pins these days.'

'No problem,' Abigail said, enunciating clearly, 'you can't be too careful, love. But next time somebody shoves a card through, just check they're who they say they are before you open the door to them—even the police.'

She was a big woman, huge and pillowy soft, with the ruin of a face and her dusty grey hair done up in an ancient pompadour style. Following her painful progress, they entered her over-heated, over-furnished sitting-room, redolent of dusty old upholstery, used air, ancient meals, old person and cat. As if this was not enough, overlying it all was the musty-sweet patchouli scent of pot-pourri, emanating from several large baskets on a table occupying the space in the bay window. A big tabby snoozed in the middle of it all, waking up from time to time to sneeze. In front of the table stood Mrs Kitchener's sagging, cushioned chair, into which she lowered her bulk with obvious relief when Mayo, envisaging the time and trouble this would take, politely declined her offer of tea.

'You'll excuse me while I get on with this,' she said. 'It's for the Rheumatism and Arthritis to sell for charity.' The old woman was already working away, deftly filling small cotton drawstring bags, baskets and straw containers of various kinds with the dried petals and spices from the baskets. 'Carry on, I can talk while I work! Sit where I can see your faces though, I don't hear so well these days.'

She was more than willing to answer the questions Abigail put to her about Angie Robinson. A visit from the police she evidently regarded as a diversion of the highest order. Settling down for a pleasurable gossip after preliminaries about how long she'd lived here—twenty-odd years—and how the neighbourhood had changed—gone downhill and no mistake—she said, 'I quite hoped somebody young would take the flat when old Dick that used to live upstairs died. Always handy, to have somebody young nearby when you can't get around much—and since my Arnold was taken . . . Well, I never thought it'd be *her*!'

'So you knew Miss Robinson before she came to live here?' Mayo asked.

'Oh yes. Well, knew who she was, at any rate. She works on the desk in the outpatients up the Women's Hospital. Dr Freeman sends me up there for my regular appointments, snotty little madam she is. That Angie Robinson, I mean, not Dr Freeman! She's lovely, always got time to listen. Can't understand how they come to be so friendly. I dare say the doctor took pity on her. She doesn't seem to have many friends. Been here six weeks and the only one I've ever seen was that chap in the big car last night—apart from the doctor, that is. "It'll be nice for you to have Angie upstairs, Mrs Kitchener," she says to me. "If you're in trouble just ring her bell and she'll look after you." Likely, I don't think! Only person she'll ever look after is Number One!'

A pause for a laboured breath enabled Mayo to get in, 'What time was this, when the man in the car came?'

'Let me see. About eight, I reckon. Yes, *The Bill* was just coming on when I heard a car draw up outside and some-body walk across the hall to her door—a man's walk. You can tell. Heavy, it was. So I peeped round the curtain and saw the car. Lucky to have found a space, he was.'

'What sort of car was it?'

'Oh Lord, don't ask me! I wouldn't know one car from t'other, specially in the dark, but it took up a lot of space, I do know that. And it was dark-coloured. Dark blue, or green, maybe black. Then, about half an hour later, I heard him come downstairs again and he rang my bell.'

'What did he look like?'

'I kept the chain on so I didn't see him clearly, but he was big. And spoke very la-di-dah and impatient, like he was used to giving orders. As if he was talking to the maid. "I had an appointment with the person upstairs at eight," he says. "The door was open so I've been waiting inside for half an hour but there's still no sign of anyone." I said mebbe she'd forgotten, or else been held up, because I'd seen her go out in that fancy white car of hers about seven o'clock. "You saw who?" he asks, sharpish. "Why, Miss Robinson!" I told him. "Who else?" "Miss Robinson," he repeats, as if he'd never heard the name before. And then he laughed, as if something had struck him as funny. "Miss Robinson? Oh yes, you mean Angie! Well, give Angie a message from me when she comes in, will you? Just tell her I couldn't wait." I asked him what his name was but he laughed again and said she'd know who it was.'

'He said the door to the flat was open when he arrived?'

'Yes, and he left it like that. I wasn't very happy about it, but I didn't pull it to because it's a Yale and I thought she might have forgotten her key—but before I went to bed I went to have another look and it was shut then, so I knew she'd come back.'

'You're sure it was her you saw go out—about seven, you said?'

'Near enough seven—I knew it was her all right, though she had her red jacket over her head to keep the rain off —her in her mini-skirt, mutton dressed as lamb!'

'You didn't hear her return?'

'No, but I don't always. She's very quiet, I'll give her that. Funny thing, though, I noticed her car wasn't outside this morning when I drew my curtains—and there was enough parking space, for a wonder.'

So where, thought Mayo, was that car now?

Having tightened the knot on the last drawstring and finished it with a neat bow, the old woman rubbed her fingers together and gave her visitors an astute look. 'Well, you haven't come here to ask me all these questions about Angie Robinson without good reason. What's she been up to, then?'

Mayo told her.

'My word,' she said after a moment's silence, 'that'll teach you to keep your tongue to yourself, Ivy Kitchener. Speaking ill of the dead!'

'You've been a lot of help to us,' Abigail reassured her. 'We need to know all we can about Miss Robinson before we can find out who killed her. You wouldn't want that sort of thing to happen to anybody else, would you?'

'Not even to her, poor thing, I wouldn't. But I can't tell you any more about her than I've already done.' She brushed bits of stalk and dried petals from her skirt and the cat, sensing the job was finished, yawned and stretched and leaped on to her lap. 'Sure you won't have a cup of tea before you go, m'duck?'

The cup of tea was declined with thanks, but before they left Mayo felt obliged to fork out generously for the charity, despite a jaundiced certainty that this wasn't an allowable expense that could be claimed.

CHAPTER 9

It was only the second post-mortem Abigail had attended. She hadn't disgraced herself by fainting at the first, and she didn't at this one—but only by the grace of God. A moment longer and her self-control would certainly have been in question, not to mention the loss of her breakfast.

'That's better,' Mayo said, filling his lungs deeply with air that was mercifully free of formaldehyde and other, less acceptable odours. Coming out into the sunshine with relief, as if he, too, was trying to dispel the reek of the mortuary which Abigail knew would persist in her nostrils for the rest of the day, and in her clothes until she'd changed them. She suspected he knew how she was feeling and was letting her down lightly. 'Your first time, is it?'

'Second, actually.'

'Well, it doesn't get any better. Well done, at least you didn't pass out.'

Basking in his approval, she smiled, beginning to feel less in awe of his seniority and more at ease.

They were emerging from the shrubbery which had been discreetly planted to screen the mortuary building from the public gaze as he spoke. Suddenly he halted, swearing under his breath. Following his glance, she glimpsed a female figure in an ankle-length trench coat lurking near the entrance to the car park, accompanied by another, probably male, with cameras slung over his shoulder.

'Come on, this way,' Mayo said, grabbing her arm. 'Coward I may be, and I'll no doubt have to face these media persons sooner or later, but for the moment I prefer to let the Press Officer deal with them. We'll walk across the park.' Turning away quickly, hopefully before they had been seen, he hurried her behind the buildings and along a path which led in a roundabout way out of the County Hospital grounds. 'I'll send someone else to pick the car up later. God, that was a lucky escape!'

Abigail laughed and followed him through the pleasant, well-kept little park which abutted on to the hospital grounds. Although it was cold and the wind was ruffling the water on the small lake where her father used to bring her to feed the ducks, and though the branches were still bare, the sour green buds of the daffodils were just about to burst and crocus had spread themselves in sheets under the trees. Ducks were quacking, children rolled balls across the grass, the sun was trying to break through from behind the clouds and Mayo, who was not famously noted for his charm, was going out of his way to be nice to her. Abigail felt herself begin to relax for the first time that morning. For the first time since last night's argument, if the truth be told . . .

She tried to dismiss thoughts of last night but the letter from the house agent, crackling in her pocket, wouldn't let her. He was pestering her for a decision on a small house just outside Brome, and wrote now that there were other people interested. A self-interested lie, she was certain, but she was going to have to make up her mind, anyway, for several other reasons. At the moment, she was living with her parents, though it wasn't a state of affairs considered permanent or desirable by any of them. Indeed, her mother's quickly-concealed dismay at the thought of such had been comic, when her daughter had come home after university and her initial police training. Abigail had been born relatively late in their lives and the two of them, her mother and father, had grown used to being a pair again, to the gentle routine of their lives in retirement—her mother's bridge and meals-on-wheels, her father's Spanish classes. That was one reason. And to Abigail, having her own space was one of the most important things in life, which was another reason—and the cause of the argument last night.

She desperately wanted the house, but she was determined it was going to be hers alone.

She'd fallen for it immediately, but its semi-derelict condition and her own lack of time, plus a reluctance to saddle herself with a mortgage, was making her hold back. What attracted her as much as anything was its garden. You could do a lot with a garden. You could have fun taking out your frustrations on a stint of deep digging, or heaving stones around to make a rockery. You could lie back and drink lemonade on the patio. Grow roses. And your own veg, fresh as the morning dew. Also, let it not be forgotten, mow the lawn, trim the hedges, chase bugs with a spray, weed the vegetable patch . . . it needed thinking about, if you were a CID officer and your free time didn't come on a regular, or even dependable, basis. And if you had ambition. She sighed and forced her thoughts back to her job, to what, in the end, mattered most to her.

'Not what we expected from the PM, was it, sir?' she ventured as an opening gambit after a moment or two.

'That's what PMs are allegedly for—so we shan't be tempted to take anything for granted—in theory, at least.'

The pathologist had made his expected pronouncements: that death was due to manual strangulation; that the scratches on the dead woman's neck were defensive wounds, the minute fragments of skin underneath the nails were her own, made by herself when she had clawed at her assailant in an attempt to save herself, thereby breaking off two of her long red fingernails. Horrible, thought Abigail, hideous thoughts of that moment of death coming unbidden. As Timpson-Ludgate had previously stated, post-mortem lividity of the body showed that it had been placed in a seated position for some time after death, probably, as he had suggested, in the seat of a car.

And then, the unexpected . . .

Despite her disordered clothing when she was found, it was quite clear that Angie Robinson had been neither raped nor sexually assaulted. Not only that, she had never at any time had sexual intercourse. She had, indisputably, been a virgin.

'One of Lavenstock's silent minority.'

That had been one of Timpson-Ludgate's tasteless jokes. Mayo didn't respond and Abigail, recalling with a shiver that icy white apartment, the array of clothes and the seductive underwear, had not found it amusing, either. She had looked with pity at the blemished face under the pathologist's scalpel, for which all the lotions, creams and unguents in the world had ultimately been of no help at all. She felt angry at the undeservedness of it, but fiercely glad the woman hadn't had to go through that final humiliation. Death, at least, must have been quick.

'He was disturbed and didn't succeed in raping her, so he strangled her to keep her quiet,' she said. There was an edge to her voice.

'Or that was what we were meant to think,' Mayo said. 'That it was a sex killing that went wrong, so that we shouldn't look for the real reason she was killed.' Abigail looked thoughtful. 'And that means,' he went on, 'that we're looking for someone, anyone, young or old . . . but someone cool and calculated enough to try an immediate cover-up. Don't forget—all the evidence indicates she was simply dumped there after being killed elsewhere. And after finding that letter, I don't see this as a casual sex killing, I think we must look closer to home.'

'Jenny Platt's checked out McKinley,' Abigail said. 'If he was in the motorway café at nine o'clock talking to other truckers, as he says he was, he's off the hook.'

'I think in any case we're looking for someone closer to home than McKinley.'

'The man who came to the flat?'

'He'll do to start with.'

They had by now arrived at the entrance to the small group of buildings which constituted the Women's

Hospital. The two hospitals, the County and the Women's, were separated only by the distance across the park. It would have been less than a five-minute drive from the County Hospital mortuary, had it not been for the allegedly quicker one-way system which took you all round the houses and left you twenty minutes later within a few yards of where you'd started. But although in terms of time they'd saved something, otherwise it didn't seem as though they'd gained much: others of the press were here also, having already ferreted out, God knows how, for there hadn't yet been a release, that the murdered woman was Angie Robinson and that she had worked here. Taking advantage of the media presence to gain publicity, a picket had been posted at the gate, a group of young nurses with protest placards which read *Women for Women* and sundry other slogans of a similar nature.

With a sigh, Mayo passed them and began to force his way through the pack, 'No comment' on his lips. He sometimes felt that he must, unknown to himself, exude some substance like aniseed, that enabled the media hounds to sniff him out wherever he went.

The name tag on the lapel of her white overall said 'Eileen Dalton'. She was a plump woman in her forties with fading, gingerish hair and tired eyes, but her face lit up when she smiled. She was one of two receptionists on duty at the Outpatients' desk at the Women's Hospital.

'I can give you ten minutes,' she said. 'I'm due for my lunch-break now, anyway, while it's quiet. Sorry I can't take you anywhere private, but we can get a cup of tea round the corner while we talk. There won't be many there now.'

'Round the corner' proved to be a refreshment bar at the end of a corridor manned by the WVS and at the moment free of customers. Mayo and Mrs Dalton took a table by the window where presently Abigail joined them, bearing three polystyrene beakers of tea and a packet of coconut creams. Rich aromas of stew, boiled cabbage and fish wafted along the corridor.

Abigail broke open the biscuits and offered the packet to Mrs Dalton, who shook her head. 'Thanks, but I wouldn't want to spoil my lunch.'

'Meals good here?' Mayo asked.

'So-so. As good as you can expect, given the equipment they have to work with.'

'They tell me the kitchens are very up-to-date at the County, and the cuisine's up to four-star class,' he offered casually, risking a surmise and hoping it was somewhere within the bounds of probability. 'Or is that a sore subject?'

'Not at all!' She shook her head, smiling. 'Never let it be said, in these hallowed premises at least, but I'm all for the change. Better facilities than here—and not so strapped for room. We're quiet at the moment but you should see it when the clinics start! Absolute Bedlam, sometimes. This afternoon we have two, Miss Clancy's fertility clinic and Dr Freeman's family planning, both having to share the same waiting area.' Her smile, lopsided, included Abigail. 'Funny old world sometimes, isn't it?'

'Gets funnier by the day,' Abigail agreed drily. 'Especially if you're female. How long have you and Angie Robinson worked together?'

'Since I started here, a couple of years ago. She'd been here for ages, though—she was practically an institution.'

'Get to know her well, did you?'

'I don't think anybody knew her very well, except perhaps for her friend, Dr Freeman. Her only friend, I shouldn't wonder!'

'A pretty unusual sort of friendship, wasn't it?' Mayo asked. 'Attraction of opposites?'

'I don't know. She was one of the doctor's lame ducks, I think. And give Angie her due, she would've done anything for Dr Freeman. Lately, since they got this protest going . . . I can't imagine what the doctor's going to do about that, now. I know she's the motivating force behind it, but Angie was doing the organizing, everybody had to consult her before anything was done, which was of course meat and drink to her . . .' Mrs Dalton gave them both a quick glance, looked a little shamefaced and said, 'You'll gather from all this that she wasn't my favourite person. To tell you the truth, she got on my nerves, always moaning about something or other, though what she had to moan about I don't know. I got fed up with listening to her. I'm what they call a one-parent family, I've got three teenagers and a full-time job and I needed her problems like I need a hole in the head.'

'You have my sympathies,' Mayo said. 'People like that can be hard to take. But cast your mind back, if you can, and try to recall if she ever said anything about some new accommodation she was interested in?'

Mrs Dalton stared. 'She'd just moved into a new flat, hadn't she?'

'It seems she regarded that as only temporary.'

'Did she? Well, I suppose she would, seeing it was on Bulstrode Street. A bit of a come-down from Kilbracken Road.'

'She may have had an appointment to view another place. Did she ever mention that? Or talk of anyone she was going to see about it—some man, maybe?'

The receptionist absent-mindedly stirred another spoonful of sugar into her tea and frowned. 'She may have done. But not that I recall.'

'Did she ever, as far as you remember, talk about her past life? People she'd met?'

'Gracious, no! When we did talk—which wasn't often, not much time—the usual topic of conversation centred around her leaving here. Not that she was ever likely to.'

Ever sensitive to a possible lead, Mayo's nose twitched. Mrs Dalton explained: 'This job's not exactly brain-taxing, which is why I like it, it keeps my mind free for other things, but Angie . . . well, I didn't like her, but I have to admit she was wasted here, though I think it was all talk on her part about leaving. She was a bit of a romancer, you know, you couldn't always believe what she said—but she wasn't as feather-brained as she let you think. Very sharp, really. I reckon she could easily have got herself something better, if she'd wanted.'

'So why do you think she didn't? Why stay here?'

'She was in charge of Reception here—big deal, as my kids say. Case of a big fish in a little pond, I suppose.' She broke off, biting her lip as she looked at her watch, pushing aside what was left of her tea and reaching for her bag on the floor beside her. 'I'm sorry, I'm being bitchy, the woman is dead, after all.'

'Give us a few more minutes, Mrs Dalton, and then we'll let you get off to your lunch. Were you both working here yesterday?'

'That's right, until five o'clock.'

'Did you leave together?'

'Yes, she didn't have her umbrella with her and we shared mine to the car park—you know what the weather was like yesterday. And you know, it's funny, you say she was murdered last night? Well, I saw her drive off, but her car was there this morning in its usual space, next to mine, when I arrived.'

It still was. A new white Ford Astra, and if it had been driven in the rain of the previous day, it had certainly been put through a car wash since. On the back seat was a red wool jacket, still slightly damp within the folds.

CHAPTER 10

Kitty Wilbraham, born Kitty Everett in 1901. In 1925, married Dr Alfred Wilbraham, who died in 1939. No children. Spalding's presentation was rather like the man himself, workmanlike and competent, laconic, neatly put together, but with a lot of subtext underneath. He was routinely put on to this sort of inquiry because he could be guaranteed to do a thorough and reliable job, but in this instance it had been at Mayo's specific direction. He couldn't afford to take him off the investigation altogether but felt he would work better at one remove—any personal involvement, however remote, had to be taken into consideration, and there were undercurrents in Spalding's domestic life, possible family complications that couldn't be allowed to get in the way of the smooth working of the investigation. He read on. *Worked until the outbreak of war with her husband on the excavations at Carthage, near Tunis. Employed in secret work at the War Office during the war, and afterwards published several books (listed below). Between 1946 and 1970 she lived in North Africa. In 1970, she returned again to England and settled at Flowerdew, her house near Morwen. Stayed there until 1979, when she was reported to have returned once more to live in the city of Tunis.*

So this was the woman Sophie Lawrence had worked for. (Sophie Amhurst she'd been then, now Lawrence, though divorced, with Sophie something else in between.) Mayo shuffled the papers together, finished his coffee and went to join Abigail Moon, who was waiting to drive him out to Pennybridge. Poking his head in at the incident room on his way out, he made known his intended whereabouts to Atkins over the cacophony of telephones, printers and other people's raised voices, and before Cherry could catch him for another update on the case, escaped.

After buckling on his seat-belt and settling down while Abigail negotiated the entrance into Milford Street, he quickly read through the notes for her benefit. 'So, there's plenty known about Mrs Wilbraham until 1979—and you'll note that was fourteen years ago,' he remarked. 'But since then—zilch.'

'So it looks fairly conclusive that she was the old woman who was killed? At any rate, she's certainly disappeared into thin air. And she *did* work on the ruins at Carthage, wrote books about it, too, which ties in with all those peculiar references to the cremation urns and so on. But—'

'But what? Doubts, Abigail?'

'Well, anyone who writes a letter like that must be more than a bit disturbed, wouldn't you say? And Mrs Dalton did say she was a bit of a romancer.'

'So we'd better take it all with a pinch of salt? I'd go along with that—up to a point. But what if Angie wasn't just another nutcase? She was also smart, if a bit hysterical, so maybe she was simply telling the truth in her own garbled way. If we extract the nub of it from all the flim-flam, what it says is that Kitty Wilbraham was killed by some man in a fit of temper, and that Angie was very likely a witness to it.'

'And Dido? Dido-Elissa? Was that part of the flimflam as well?'

'Not altogether, but I don't think we should let it smoke-screen the main facts. And with either a bit of luck or a lot of persuasion, Sophie Lawrence is going to be able to tell us what they were.'

He has his own ideas, Abigail said to herself, he's sussed that one out. And he's not telling me, either because he feels I ought to be able to work it out for myself or else he's going to bring it out later, like a rabbit from a hat, the great Sherlock. The latter attitude was a ploy she'd come across before but she didn't yet know whether that sort of thing was Mayo's form.

'A more immediate question,' the DCI went on, unaware of these interesting speculations on his character, 'is how did Angie Robinson come to be involved with Kitty Wilbraham in the first place?'

'Sophie should be able to tell us that, too. We've struck lucky, it seems, finding her at home—finding her in England at all, in fact.'

At the moment Mayo felt he wouldn't be averse to a bit of luck. Fast approaching was his own private three-day limit, the deadline that always seemed to divide the easily sewn-up case from the one likely to drag on for months, the sort that clung on to your back like an old man of the sea. Easy, easy, he told himself. Yet impatience seethed in him to get things going, not to allow them to stagnate to the point where disinterest on the part of all concerned might set in. As if to underline his frustration, he became aware of the car slowing down. 'What's all this?' he demanded, their progress becoming further halted when the line of cars ahead slowed to a crawl and finally stopped altogether.

'Seems to be an obstruction ahead,' Abigail said, rolling down the window and craning her neck out.

They came marching down the middle of the road in their crisp uniforms, starched caps and aprons, red capes, sensible black lace-ups doing nothing even for those with the best of legs. Latter-day Nightingales, though not too many of them, since half their number at least would be on duty at the Women's Hospital. Followed by present-day feminists, banner-carrying supporters, committed free-thinkers, anti-government protesters. High school sixth-formers, rattling tins, handing out leaflets. Mothers with toddlers and babies in prams. Nearly a hundred women in all, stopping the traffic and chanting their theme like some Greek chorus, gaped at and occasionally cheered on by the shopping crowds.

Heading the procession was Madeleine Freeman. Tall and with her head lifted, purposeful in her stride—so, Mayo thought, must Joan of Arc have looked, or Mrs Pankhurst. He watched with admiration, for a moment finding it in his heart to envy the man she was going to marry. The feeling was transitory. He very well knew that such single-mindedness in a partner would frighten the life out of him, a view already expressed about the doctor by more than one man working on the case. Hardly comfortable to live with—not exactly a warm armful on a winter's night was the general opinion.

'Good Lord,' Mayo said, a moment later. 'There's Sheila Kite.'

Sheila saw him peering out of the window and gave him a cheerful wave. He wondered if Kite knew where she was, or if his wife had taken advantage of his absence to play hookey from her job and join in the protest. On second thoughts he dismissed the latter possibility. Sheila Kite had a complete absence of guile and possessed in addition the enviable trait of being able to do and think independently, without stirring up marital discord, despite the fact that she and Kite didn't always think alike. If all these women were like Sheila and Dr Freeman, he thought wryly, the authorities might just as well throw in the towel.

The line of cars began to move again as the procession turned in at the gates of the old Hill Street Methodist chapel, a dismal building long since dissociated from its original function, now rented out for anything from flea-markets to carpet sales or the occasional rock concert, and now the hospital campaign headquarters.

'Have we finished checking with these women working on this lark?' Mayo asked. 'They'd all have known Angie Robinson.'

'So far none of them have reported seeing her on Tuesday. They rent the chapel only for three nights a week—

Monday, Wednesday and Friday, so nobody was there that night.'

He would have expected them to be working flat out, now that the closure of the Women's Hospital was imminent. Fund-raising appeals had penetrated as far as Milford Road station, where one of the WPCs had even tried to sell him tickets for an indoor barbecue and barn dance this coming weekend. He'd given her the price and told her to sell the tickets to someone else. Ninety-nine per cent of the women in the town seemed comprehensively for Dr Freeman and her campaign, and prepared to argue for it at the drop of a hat—he suspected Abigail might at that very moment be expecting him to ask for her views on the subject but he'd no desire to go down that particular path at the moment, or to be distracted from the subject of Sophie Lawrence.

She obligingly accepted the change of subject when he returned to it. 'Apparently she travels for most of the year, sir,' she responded, driving them towards Pennybridge with some style, now that they were clear of the town.

'What does she do for a living?'

'I'm not sure she does anything. She owns Oundle's Bookshop at the top of Denbigh Street, although someone else runs it for her.' She was frowning as she gave him a brief rundown on what she knew of the independent circumstances of Sophie Lawrence and her sister, Roz Spalding. 'As far as I know, Sophie's never really worked. Her sister used to teach maths at the High School, but she's given it up and become an Open University tutor.'

'You're remarkably well informed.'

For some reason Abigail looked embarrassed at this, giving him a quick, sideways glance before turning her eyes back to the road ahead and keeping them strictly there. 'Thank you, sir,' she answered politely, but her neat profile had taken on a set look, as though it was not a compliment she was pleased to receive. From then on she was silent unless spoken to until they reached the Green at

Pennybridge and spotted the tall, pink brick house they were looking for, outside which an expensive-looking red Datsun was parked. 'Drive on round the corner and we'll walk back,' Mayo instructed.

Women could, he thought as they walked towards the house, be the very devil to deal with. The experience of having Abigail working with him was—well, enlightening. He liked her direct common-sense approach, and perhaps even her intuition, a hitherto despised and considerably overrated function in his book, but he found the feminine nuances hard to keep up with. Was it something he'd said? Or something to do with Sophie Lawrence? The set of Ms Moon's lips might well mean that she disapproved of the other woman's superficial lifestyle, he thought, having already recognized in Abigail a streak of that same inherited Puritan work ethic he himself was alternately blessed and cursed with.

The brick house had a shiny, black-painted door and sported a highly-polished brass knocker. A brisk rat-tat brought an answer almost immediately, in the person of an energetic-looking young woman in hip- and thigh-hugging black leggings and an oversized, paint-stained man's shirt she'd belted round the waist, leaving her looking vaguely like some extra in a B film about mediæval Florence. Assistant to Leonardo, perhaps. 'Oh, right,' she replied cheerfully to Abigail's announcement of who they were, and her request to see Mrs Lawrence. 'Hang on, I'll tell her you're here.'

In a few moments they found themselves seated in a large drawing-room at the back of the house, a room whose pale gold silk walls and glowing, gold-framed prints gave it the appearance of floating in sunlight, although the day outside was grey and overcast. Elegant, eighteenth-century furnishings, stiff and formal to Mayo's way of thinking. Not a thing out of line, every chair, table or cabinet a period piece. It was the sort of ambience he was ill at ease with.

It was out of his class for one thing, but anyway he preferred things gathered together haphazardly, with undemanding comfort as the prime requirement.

Sophie Lawrence came in, as elegant and expensive as the furnishings, and with the same delicate look, as if she might break if treated too roughly. She must have been very young at the time she worked for Kitty Wilbraham. Even now she looked barely thirty, a woman of nervous gestures with thin fingers and wrists seeming hardly adequate to support the quantities of gold jewellery jangling around them, wearing a mole-coloured suede skirt and a soft amethyst sweater. Her huge hazel eyes held an uncertain vulnerability, yet despite this, she spoke with self-assurance, quickly and a little huskily, and her smile had a fleeting charm. Abigail, instantly aware of designer clothes and a subtle scent she couldn't identify, was conscious of her own favourite, hitherto perfectly acceptable suit and matching silk shirt being actually nothing much to write home about.

Mrs Lawrence wasn't surprised to see them. She made the right, conventional noises but she had already heard the news from her sister.

'How can I help you? Not very much, I should think. I haven't seen Angie for fourteen years.' Said with a smile. Charming and delightful, willing to help . . . and yet, Mayo felt they were not really welcome, that the visit was looked upon as an ill-mannered intrusion, which he supposed it probably was.

'Fourteen years?' he repeated, essaying a smile. 'I'm impressed. Not many people can be so precise about when they last saw someone, especially after that length of time.'

'I'm able to say exactly, because I last saw her just about the time I stopped working for Mrs Wilbraham. That was how I met Angie, when she visited Kitty—Mrs Wilbraham.'

'What was their association?'

'Kitty knew her through Madeleine Freeman, whose friend she was. Madeleine was Kitty's doctor, and Angie used to come to Flowerdew with her.'

The connections were slotting into place. He asked in what capacity Mrs Lawrence had worked for Mrs Wilbraham.

'I was supposed to be her secretary. She'd been a famous archæologist in her time and she was writing her memoirs.' She made a deprecatory gesture, smiling faintly, sitting lightly on the edge of her seat. For all that she seemed so much in tune with her affluent surroundings, with her expensive clothes, jewellery and scent, she had the uncertainty and impermanence of a bird of passage, feathers ruffled and a little battered by the voyage, not quite as young as she had at first appeared. 'I have to admit I wasn't a very good secretary, but Kitty didn't mind. It was more important to her to have someone *simpatico* . . . you know, someone she could share a joke with, someone on the same wavelength.'

His dark glance rested on her face, reading it. 'I can appreciate it would be important to have someone you can get on with in the circumstances.'

'It was more than that, we were friends from the word go. But you couldn't *not* get on with Kitty. She was a darling— and such fun.' Bending over an arrangement of cream hothouse lilies in a topaz glass bowl on the low table in front of her, she tweaked off a tiny, yellowing leaf, the slender fingers not quite steady. When she looked up, he saw her eyes bright with unshed tears. They were golden brown, like dark amber. 'I was devastated,' she went on, blinking rapidly, 'when she suddenly decided to call off writing the memoirs and go back to Tunisia, though on reflection it was understandable. For one thing, the climate was better for her health. Flowerdew—the house where she lived— was damp, and it was never warm in the winter.' As if actually feeling the remembered chill, she shivered and moved closer to the fire, wrapping her arms round herself for warmth, despite the soft cashmere she was enveloped in. It was a self-protective gesture, gauche and school-girlish, yet she managed to invest it with grace.

'She suddenly decided to leave, you say? Didn't she give you any warning? It must have taken some time to wind up her affairs.'

'No, when I went in one morning, she told me what she'd decided to do. She gave me a cheque for my salary and that was that.'

'Rather surprising behaviour, surely?'

'Not if you knew Kitty. She was very impetuous. And she loved North Africa. She'd lived and worked near Tunis for a large part of her life and missed it very much.'

'Presumably you've kept contact?'

She hesitated. 'She didn't leave an address.' She had an unconsciously annoying habit of twisting her gold bracelets round and round as she spoke. 'Actually, I wrote several times but had no answer, so naturally . . .'

Mayo waited, saying nothing.

'She was old, you know,' she said defensively. 'She was seventy-seven when she left England, and that was in 1979. I could only assume she must have died.'

He watched Abigail note this down before continuing. 'Tell me, did you live in, at Flowerdew?'

'Sometimes I stayed the night, if we were working late, but mostly I went home. My sister wasn't married then and I lived with her.'

'Who else lived at the house?'

'The housekeeper, Jessie Crowther.'

'And nobody else?'

'Not on a permanent basis.' Twisting her bangles, she added, 'But there were always lots of visitors. Kitty liked to have people staying with her.'

'You say Angie Robinson used to come with Dr Freeman

on her visits to Mrs Wilbraham. That's a bit unusual, isn't
it?'

'Not really. Madeleine was more than just her doctor—
she was a very good friend. And of course she didn't bring
Angie with her when she called professionally—only when
she visited socially. Kitty didn't mind . . . as I've said,
anyone was welcome at Flowerdew.'

'What sort of a house was it?'

The abrupt change of direction made her blink but he
had the feeling that it was not a change she welcomed, any
more than the previous conversation. 'An old house, with
a lake in front, and a little island,' she said after an interval,
'but it's impossible to describe it. You'd have to see it to
really appreciate what it was like, you know?'

He said easily, 'Oh, I can probably imagine it. I know
what these people who've lived abroad for most of their life
are like. A famous archæologist like Mrs Wilbraham, I
expect the house was stuffed with mementoes of her work,
artefacts and so on?'

'No,' she said shortly. 'It wasn't. Kitty couldn't legally
have brought the genuine thing out of Tunisia—the only
things she had were replicas brought home by herself and
her husband, and they were all kept in the one room. Some
of them were rather grisly and apt to make people feel
uncomfortable, so she'd had an extension built on, the room
where she worked, especially to house them. They weren't
for public viewing.'

'Masks, perhaps? Cremation urns?'

She sat up just that much straighter, surprised and distinctly wary, a tinge of pink shading each high cheekbone.
'Yes, she did have some things like that in her workroom.
But otherwise Flowerdew was furnished just like any other
house. But what is all this about Kitty and her home? I
thought it was Angie Robinson you were interested in?'

'Well, you see, Mrs Lawrence, Angie Robinson left a
record of something that happened there that seemed to

have upset her, and although it was apparently some time since, we have to investigate anything at all that might have some bearing on her death. You do see that?'

'Of course I see it,' she returned quickly. 'But Angie was a hysterical type, it didn't take much to upset her.' She paused. 'What sort of record? What did she say had happened?' It was as if she held her breath while he answered.

'A seance, for instance,' he suggested, avoiding a direct answer. 'That would be the sort of thing that would upset her?'

He'd scored a bull's eye there, Abigail thought, and saw at once how that might be the explanation of the puzzling phrase in the letter Angie had written. *The night she died, Dido came . . . there were bad vibes . . . death for the old woman.* The spirit of Dido-Elissa. A seance. Of course.

But Sophie Lawrence was frowning, pale face now even paler, and her soft mouth pulled in tight, professing not to understand. 'A seance? What can you mean?'

'A sort of gathering where I understand the spirits of the dead are called up.'

'I know what a seance is—but we certainly never had one at Flowerdew! I can't think what put that into your mind.'

'Can't you? Well, never mind,' Mayo said. 'It's just a point that I expect I can clear up. So, it's fourteen years since you last saw Angie Robinson? And you haven't been in touch with each other since?'

'Angie and I?' One delicate eyebrow was raised, signifying incredulity. 'There would have been absolutely no reason for us to do so. We weren't friends, just acquaintances who met occasionally. We'd simply nothing in common.'

'You didn't see her on Tuesday evening, then?'

'No, I did not. On Tuesday evening I was here at home, after about half past six, that is. Earlier, I went to see my sister with a present for my nephew, who's in hospital at the moment. I came home and watched TV for a while, then went to bed early to read. I heard Maggie come in about ten but she has her own key and went straight to her room.'

'Maggie?' Mayo said, when Abigail had noted the relevant times. 'Would that be the girl who let us in? Does she work for you?'

'No, she's a friend, a painter who uses the attic floor as a studio. Sometimes, when I'm away, she lives in the house. As she is doing at the moment.'

'I'd like to have a word with Maggie.'

'She's gone out again, didn't you hear her bang the door? Today's her day for teaching at the Poly. And now—' she glanced at the tiny gold wristwatch hiding among the brace-lets and rose to her feet in one lovely, fluid movement—'if that's all, Chief Inspector, I do have an appointment to have my hair washed in a few minutes. It's only round the corner but André doesn't like his clients to keep him waiting.'

'Thank you, Mrs Lawrence. We'll be in touch later but I think that *is* all for the moment.'

'Well, certainly, if you think there's anything else I can do, please don't hesitate to contact me.'

Her smile was bright, brittle, social.

How to be the gracious lady in one easy lesson. Like dis-missing the bloody gardener, Mayo thought, as they walked back to the cul-de-sac where they had parked, furious with himself for minding. He thought he had lost that kind of sensitivity with his constable's boots, but some people still had the ability to get under his skin. He'd accepted the dismissal because for the moment, there wasn't anything more to be gained from questioning Sophie Lawrence. He felt very strongly that the real woman hadn't been much in evidence, that the sophisticated veneer concealed a woman who was maybe unsure but maybe not. Certainly more than a little frightened. That most of what she'd told them and been rehearsed, that there were several things she hadn't told them, and the only thing to do would be to come back when she was less prepared.

'As a woman, what's your impression of Mrs Lawrence?' he asked Abigail.

Abigail thought for a moment. 'As a woman, I'd say she's not very happy. Perhaps because she's not living up to her potential.' She flushed slightly, grinned and said, 'In words of one syllable, she's nobody's fool, is she?'

'Quite the opposite.'

'And all she's doing with her life is frittering it away.'

'As far as we know,' he said, giving her a sharp look.

'As far as we know,' she agreed evenly.

When they reached the car, he said, 'Radio for another car, Abigail, to come and pick me up, then you can drive down to the Poly and see what you can get from this girl Maggie.'

CHAPTER 11

Oundle's Bookshop was a good place to be on a miserable early afternoon, the sort of shop where customers were actually encouraged to browse by a scatter of comfortable chairs set about at strategic points. The interior was warm, and the books on offer were interesting. Classical music tapes played unobtrusively in the background. In addition, the rear of the shop sported a well-patronized small coffee corner which sold Viennese pastries, homemade biscuits and slices of pie. It had been run for the last eight or nine years by a husband and wife called Conran. It was one of Alex Jones's favourite places for relaxing when she was off duty. She was known as a good customer and greeted with pleasure by the Conrans. She had just brought a couple of paperbacks and a travel book and was sitting back with a cup of the most delicious coffee to be found in Lavenstock. Alex hadn't Mayo's ear for music; she wasn't passionate about it, but under his tuition her musical tastebuds were coming alive and she was learning to savour classical music rather than gulp it down as medicine. She was surprised and delighted to recognize the Beethoven string quartet in a minor key that was being played . . . and to be able to put a name to it, what was more: F minor, Opus 95. Its slightly melancholy strains were perfectly in tune with the damp, grey day. She was flicking through one of her new acquisitions, making the most of not being in any hurry, wickedly indulging herself with a slice of delicious *Sachertorte*, when she looked up and saw Abigail Moon come in and order herself coffee.

'Come and join me,' Alex invited from her corner as the young WDC turned with her hands full and began to look for a table.

Abigail put down her plate and cup, took stock of what she could see of the rest of the shop and sat herself down on the same side of the table as Alex. 'Better sit here, where I can keep a weather eye. I've been following the woman who's just gone into the back premises.'

'Who is she?' Alex asked.

'Name of Sophie Lawrence. Earlier this morning we interviewed her, in the course of which she told us a fib about having an appointment with her hairdresser. Maybe it was just to get rid of us—the DCI was getting a bit too near the mark for comfort as far as she was concerned— but when I saw her in front of me at the traffic lights a few minutes ago, I knew she hadn't had time to get her hair done. It's nearly as long as mine,' she said, tossing the thick chestnut plait that hung between her shoulders. 'So I decided to follow her, since I'd also just found out she'd lied to us about something else, from a girl who lives with her.'

*

Abigail had found the girl alone in the art room at the Poly, in a thick fug of turps fumes and tobacco smoke, enjoying an illicit drag before her class began. Her name was Maggie Renfrew.

'Yes, I was out on Tuesday evening, from quarter to seven to about ten,' she confirmed, stubbing out her cigarette and throwing the windows wide. 'I run a couple of evening classes here every week, as well as this one.'

'So you wouldn't know if Mrs Lawrence was home all evening?'

Maggie regarded Abigail steadily. 'What does *she* say?'

'It's just a matter of confirmation. She says she was.'

'Well, then, she was.' Examining a clutch of brushes which had been stuck in a jar, the girl added, 'Anyway, she would be at home, wouldn't she, when she was entertaining a gentleman friend? Oops, not quite what I meant!'

'Who was this? Someone you know?'

'Couldn't say. I never actually saw him—only heard his voice when I passed the drawing-room door. How it was, I got half way here on my bike and then found I'd forgotten something . . . actually it was the written assessments of my students' work. They're a bind to do but the Poly decrees they must have them and the pupils are apt to get a bit shirty if I forget.' Squatting in front of a low cupboard, she began extracting piles of drawing paper, speaking over her shoulder. 'So even though it was raining cats and dogs, I shot back and that was when I saw the car outside and realized Sophie had a visitor.'

'What time would that have been?'

Maggie sat back on her heels and considered. 'It didn't take me more than a minute to dash upstairs for my papers and be off again, but I only just made it back here for half past, so it must've been about ten past, quarter past seven. The car wasn't there when I got back again, though, just before ten.'

'Was it one you'd ever seen there before?'

'No,' Maggie replied, standing up. 'But I don't clock in all her callers. None of my business.'

'Don't suppose you know what kind it was, either?'

'Well, I can't say I know much about cars, a bike being the most I can aspire to for the foreseeable future, and I was in a big rush, but I reckon even I know a Jag when I see one.'

'What about the number?'

'Not a hope. I'd never notice that, I'm numerically illiterate. I can tell you the colour, though—that's something I always notice! It was that lovely dark racing green. It might have been one of the newer models—or on the other hand, just in good nick, I wouldn't know.'

It was only a few minutes after leaving Maggie Renfrew, when Abigail was halted at a red light, that she had seen Sophie Lawrence a couple of cars ahead in the red Datsun which had been parked outside her house, and realized that she couldn't have been to the hairdresser in the time—so she'd either failed to keep the appointment, or been fibbing about having one in the first place. The lights changed and on impulse she had followed her into the car park, through the shopping centre and had finally seen her enter the bookshop, have a word with Liz Conran and go straight into the back quarters.

'I'm beginning to think I've over-reacted and she's here quite legit, but I might as well have some lunch while I'm here,' she said to Alex, tucking into a large wedge of quiche.

'A man went through to the back about fifteen minutes ago,' Alex offered. 'Then when the woman arrived Liz took coffee and cakes in for two.'

'What was he like?' Abigail was suddenly hopeful again.

'Big chap, reminded me of someone.'

'You couldn't hazard a guess who?'

'Sorry, it was only a fleeting glimpse. Someone you're interested in?'

'Could be—especially if he came in a dark green Jaguar.' She didn't expect Alex to have seen it, though, since there were double yellow lines in the street outside.

'Unlikely,' said Alex. 'He was carrying a crash helmet.'

'Oh. Oh well, I suppose she's a right to arrange her assignations here if she wants. He might even be her accountant! She owns this place, did you know?'

'No, though I knew the Conrans didn't. Does she really? She looks a bit young for that sort of caper.'

'She's older than she looks, and anyway she has money, left her by her parents. She bought it as an investment, or so Nick says.' The pause was barely perceptible. 'Nick Spalding, I mean, he's married to her sister,' she said, a little too casually.

For a while they talked station gossip. 'Any joy with your house-hunting?' Alex asked, finishing the last chocolate mouthful and pushing her plate away.

'As it happens, yes. I've seen the loveliest little house, two up, two down, kitchen added to the back, bathroom above. Not in very good shape, which is one of the reasons I can afford it, but—' Abigail broke off, tracing the chequered pattern of the cloth with her finger. 'It might not be such a good spec . . . if I had to leave quickly, for instance.'

'Leave? You haven't been here five minutes!'

'All the same, I'd move tomorrow if it meant promotion! Oh, I'm happy enough here. But there's a possibility I might *have* to move, for personal reasons.' She added after a cautious assessment of Alex, 'To do with Nick Spalding, as I think you've guessed.'

Alex had for some time been intuitively aware of the situation existing between the young Sergeant and DC Spalding, though both Abigail and Spalding himself had been careful not to make it obvious and Alex thought few others suspected. Perhaps her awareness of it sprang from the fact that it was in some way a reflection of her own circumstances. She thought Abigail had brains, ambition, and susceptibility, a dangerous combination, and that Nick Spalding was deep and difficult. Also much older than Abigail, besides being junior to her in rank. She could see trouble ahead but that was their business; they were both old enough to know the score.

She wouldn't have pursued the subject had Abigail not made it plain she wanted to talk, so she drank the last of her coffee, registered interest and waited for Abigail to go on.

The two women had struck up an immediate rapport when they'd first met and Abigail knew Alex would understand, if not sympathize with her. It wasn't really an appropriate time to broach the subject, when their talk was likely to be interrupted any minute, but Abigail was possessed of an impulsive streak, the same unthinking impulse that had started all this miserable business. She was aghast now, looking back, at how careless she'd been, how thoughtlessly she'd allowed the situation to develop, with the possibility of endangering not only her career prospects, but Nick's chances of mending his marriage. 'It wasn't because of me they split up,' she said, pushing the quiche around with her fork as though she'd all at once lost her appetite. 'They'd already parted company before we met, but it wasn't terminal. They were going through a difficult patch —she has money and he has a DC's salary and quaint old-fashioned ideas about not living beyond it. I didn't know anybody when I came here and he was at a loose end, having just left Roz . . . I suppose we gravitated to one another. Just mutual sympathy, I thought, nothing heavy. Naïve, wasn't I?' She ate some quiche, sipped some coffee and was suddenly quiet. 'There's a child,' she said at last, 'a little boy. Michael. He's six years old and he has leukæmia.'

'Abigail!'

'I know, it's diabolical. I feel savage when I think of it.' The only way was *not* to think of it any more than she could help, but this happened to be a great deal of the time. 'But just now they say he's in remission, which is marvellous. There's talk of a cure. He's coming out of hospital and of course he needs both his parents . . .'

'Naturally. But it's pretty tough on you as well.'

Abigail threw Alex an unreadable look. 'Well, Nick says he's going back to them only for Michael's sake, but he knows that she—Roz—will think it's all stations go again. And he won't admit that's what he really wants, too, though he *says* he also wants us to carry on just the same—which just isn't on, as far as I'm concerned,' she added with a return of her usual spirit.

Alex wasn't sure she understood what Abigail was driving at. She had begun to look hunted. 'He's so damned stubborn! He's convinced himself that if he goes back to her I'll be devastated, and nothing I say will make him admit otherwise. He prefers to think I'm pretending it's all over between us because I'm just being noble about Michael, rather than admit the truth.'

'Which is—?'

'That there was never much to begin with, and there's nothing left now. But there's no way of putting that one nicely.'

'Niceness is what you *don't* need in a situation like this,' Alex said bluntly, with some feeling. 'Take it from me.'

It was as near as she could go, or intended to go, towards talking about herself, but she saw that Abigail understood the oblique reference. She was very quick on the uptake, the sort of person on whom nothing was ever lost. What she couldn't possibly know was that Alex had worked through a bad relationship with one man who'd never had any intention of leaving his wife for her and immediately she'd freed herself had become involved in another, this time with Gil

Mayo. Far from bad this time, but fraught with peril, all the same. She could alter that situation in a moment, simply by saying yes, she'd marry him, but that discounted the small matter of her own ambition and their conflicting aims.

And yet . . . wasn't it, she thought suddenly, time she took another look at herself and what she really wanted? If she were totally honest, there had been opportunities lately that she had let slip. It was such an astonishing acknowledgement she felt stopped in her tracks, though Abigail didn't appear to notice the silence that fell between them.

The taped music stopped. Abigail looked up from trying to find the solution to her problems in her coffee and smiled. She had the sort of smile that lit the air around her when she was really using it. 'Thanks for listening, Alex. It's done me good to get it off my chest—though I think I probably knew what I have to do all the time.'

As she spoke a man carrying a motorcycle helmet emerged from the back premises and strode to the door. Alex said, 'That's him.'

Released, Abigail pushed aside her chair and with a quick, ''Bye!' plunged after him into the market-day crowds, leaving most of her quiche and some of her coffee untouched.

Her quarry was threading with some speed between the rows of market stalls that lay on the other side of the street. Nevertheless, she was able to keep him in view until an old lady with a basket-on-wheels suddenly swung it round from the stall where she'd been buying vegetables, catching Abigail a smart and exceedingly painful blow on the ankle and blocking the gangway between the stalls.

'Ooh, sorry love, didn't hurt you, did I?'

'Not a bit,' Abigail lied, hopping out of the way. 'No problem.' The incident had halted her no more than a few seconds, but when she refocused on the spot where the man had been a moment before, he wasn't there. He'd been near the place where the market ended and several roads came together, and he could have taken any of them, or have gone into the open air car park round the corner and by now be half way down the Coventry road. At any rate, he didn't materialize when she stationed herself at the car park exit, giving herself fifteen minutes to watch, and finally she had to admit that she'd lost him.

While Abigail was walking back to the station, filled with disconsolate thoughts and furious with herself for having lost her quarry, Alex, having finished her coffee, went to position herself near the door to the back premises, on the pretext of looking at the enticing display of cookery books in that corner. Finally, when she was sure Liz was no longer occupied with customers, she asked if she might speak to Sophie Lawrence, explaining that she had seen her go through the door marked 'Private'. After an initial hesitation Liz, knowing Alex in her capacity as police sergeant as well as customer, took her into the office. Whereupon it was discovered that Sophie had already left by the back door.

And, no doubt because the shop had private parking facilities at the rear, not only Sophie, but the second person she'd been speaking to had also left that way. For after Abigail had left in pursuit of the motorcyclist and while she, Alex, was leafing through Elizabeth David, she had distinctly heard two people talking. One had definitely been female but she couldn't have sworn to the other.

CHAPTER 12

Moses the cat was seriously displeased with Mayo, turning his back on the erstwhile object of his adoration like a wife with a headache. For weeks after Bert's arrival grey old Moses had sat outside the door of the upstairs flat with his head on one side and a puzzled expression on his face, but by now it seemed to have dawned on him that he'd been beaten in the race for Mayo's affections by a parrot—though Moses, poor unlovely cat, had never had much of a chance in the first place.

Feeling in no mood for eating police canteen food the previous night, Mayo had settled for fish and chips for supper, believing he'd be eating alone, and had opened his door and found Alex there. Supper had ceased to be a matter of importance. Later, they went out for a Chinese meal. But when he donated the unwanted piece of cod the next morning to Moses, as usual slinking about outside the upstairs flat, the cat sulkily wouldn't touch it—not if it had been Dover sole, he wouldn't.

'Don't be like that, Mosh, life's too short,' Mayo jollied him, refusing to take offence, full of the milk of human kindness, prepared to forgive even Moses on this beautiful morning. But Moses wasn't prepared to reciprocate, and he had to throw the fish into the dustbin on the way out.

His buoyant mood lasted all the way to the station, where he was greeted by Kite, back at his desk, cock-a-hoop, mission accomplished, his runaway witness found and brought back to Lavenstock. They discussed procedures for about twenty minutes. The weight of evidence gathered was enormous: enough to keep Kite busy with reports, court appearances and collating witness statements for the foreseeable future; enough to bring charges and be certain of committal proceedings—these men were going to be put away for a lot of years, if Kite had anything to do with it. Mayo had barely turned round to face the inevitable weight of paperwork landing on his own desk when he was intercepted by Atkins with further news: 'There's been another one of those break-ins.'

'Another doctor?'

This time it was the Freeman, Lall, Smith practice. 'Just like the others,' Atkins commented, 'same MO, has to be the same lot. It bears all their trademarks. We can't really spare anybody but I've sent Deeley and Jenny Platt—they've been working on the others.'

Mayo had already made up his mind that the time had come to pay Madeleine Freeman another visit. The last time he'd seen the doctor there hadn't, at that point, been anything to link Angie Robinson and the anonymous letter. But now, having established that she had written it, and having learned of Madeleine Freeman's connection with Kitty Wilbraham, it was logical to hope that Dr Freeman might be able to throw some light on the contents of the letter.

On his way out, he met Abigail, just returned from Pennybridge, where she'd been to question Sophie Lawrence about her visitor on the night of the murder. 'She denied it, of course—said the Jaguar must have belonged to someone visiting one of her neighbours—and the voice Maggie heard must have been the television.'

Mayo found Deeley and Jenny Platt had already left the surgery, having done what was necessary. The waiting-room was in even greater chaos than before, with an identical lot of whingeing tots scrapping with one another over a box of plastic toys and an identical set of young mothers looking as though they'd just about had it up to here.

Only the dragon was different, and Mayo took a perverse satisfaction in seeing that she'd gone to pieces over the break-in and was being sharply admonished for it by one of the doctors.

'Pull yourself together, Jane, it's not the end of the world.'

The speaker was a blue-eyed, russet-haired Irish beauty, who introduced herself as Dr Mary Smith. But Jane was inconsolable. 'How am I ever going to put things right again?'

'I expect you'll manage, you always do.'

'Is Dr Freeman here?' ventured Mayo.

'Oh, she's in her surgery!' returned the distracted dragon, flapping her hand towards the door. This time she didn't advise him to knock. He could have kicked the door in for all she cared.

The probability of the culprits being apprehended wasn't one Mayo could view with optimism, but he felt obliged to reassure the doctor. 'We'll let you know how things progress, Dr Freeman. Yours is just the latest in a series we've had to contend with lately, I'm afraid, but we're bound to catch them soon.'

'They won't have got much if they were looking for drugs . . . we've more sense than to keep much here.' She was philosophic about the burglary, calmly waiting for him to begin what he had patently come for. A Chief Inspector in the middle of a murder case wouldn't be concerning himself with minor break-ins.

She looked strained, even a little haggard. She kept rubbing her forehead just above the bridge of her spectacles, with the gesture that seemed to be a habit, as if she had a nagging headache. There was a distinct diminishment of that splendid bloom of health he had first noticed in her, or that air of being lit from within which had appeared to be buoying her up yesterday at the demonstration and which gave such distinction to her looks. He put it down to reaction to the shock of Angie's murder. Or perhaps she'd just been up all night; even with duty rosters and shared responsibilities, it was bound to happen in a busy practice.

'Here, let me do that,' Mayo said as she began to move a pile of campaign leaflets which stood on the edge of her desk and was obstructing her view of him. He put them where she indicated and remarked, 'I saw your demonstration yesterday. It seemed to be a success with the general public, but it must make a lot of work for you.'

'It's success with the powers-that-be that matters—and hard work doesn't come into it,' she replied simply, 'not when it's a cause you'd go to the stake for.'

She wasn't exaggerating. She really meant what she said. He hadn't been so far out, seeing her as a latter-day Joan of Arc. But such commitment took the wind out of his sails, left him breathless. Was it with admiration, or envy, because he had nothing that came within miles of this? People, yes, they mattered to him as much as that—Alex, of course, his dear love. And his daughter, that went without saying . . . But a cause, a commitment?

She must, by some trick of telepathy, have picked up his thought. Smiling faintly, she asked, 'Do you play chess?'

'Occasionally. Not very well. I'm too impatient.' Which was only partly true. He was a man patient in the extreme when it came to tracking down a villain or sifting through the details of a case. And he could spend all day regulating the most wayward and finicky of clocks, but games of any kind bored him. He lacked the competitive spirit over something he could see only as a time-wasting diversion.

'You should. It's a useful accomplishment, if only because it teaches you to plan ahead. And believe me, I've planned! I've watched and waited, and worked out my strategy so that I know exactly what moves I'm going to make. This business of the Women's Hospital's been on the agenda for years, with all sorts of schemes for and against. I once thought it might be privately financed . . . that turned out to be a pipe dream, but we're bound to win in the end, if not by sheer weight of opinion, then by more militant methods.' A sudden, rather mischievous smile illuminated her face and chased away the sententiousness. 'I shouldn't be saying this to you of all people, should I?'

'We'd better forget you did, then.'

The smile slowly died, and her eyes were shadowed again. The small frown between her brows reappeared. 'Any news yet?'

'Something has cropped up since we saw you last, yes. I think you may be able to help, at any rate I'd like to talk to you about it.'

'You've some idea who might have been responsible?'

'Oh, it's too early for that yet.' The usual soothing, ano-dyne platitude. 'We've a lot of inquiries to follow through, but first—what can you tell me about a woman called Kitty Wilbraham?'

'Kitty Wilbraham?' A little silence fell. 'She was a patient of mine—a private patient—in my previous practice.'

'How long ago would that be?'

'That's something I couldn't tell you off the cuff. But I've been here in this practice for ten years and it was before then. She went back to live in North Africa. I haven't heard of her since but I think she's almost certain to have died by now. She was nearly eighty when she left England. Does that answer your question?'

'Partly. She was a personal friend as well as a patient?'

'I hope she thought of it that way. I certainly did.'

Without elaborating further, he moved quickly on to something else, choosing his words carefully as he told her that evidence had been found suggesting that Angie Robinson had been the writer of an anonymous letter. One which might well provide a motive for her murder.

At first politely incredulous, her expression changed as he explained further. But having no alternative but to believe him, she was obviously deeply reluctant to accept that Angie had done what he said she had.

'The letter seems to refer to something that happened fourteen years ago, and seemingly upset her badly. A seance of sorts,' he said, using the word deliberately this time, since it seemed to get people going. 'Possibly at a place called Flowerdew.'

'Flowerdew! That was Kitty's house!'

'So I believe, ma'am.'

Outside in the waiting-room a child burst into a loud wail, held its breath for a perilous length of time, then started again, full force. She waited until it had been paci-fied, then said quietly, 'You're talking about that game we played, aren't you? That idiotic game? Somebody's told you, Sophie, I imagine. I can't imagine now why I ever agreed to participate.' She broke off. 'But I don't understand how something as trivial as that possibly have caused Angie's murder.'

'Trivial? Perhaps you'd better tell me about it first, before we allow that.'

'Well, it certainly wasn't a seance! Just a silly idea someone had to pass an idle hour. I don't remember whose idea it was. Fingers on a glass, pushing letters about on a table top, you know the sort of thing. It was nothing.'

'Oh, I don't know that I'd call it nothing. Some people are funny about things like that. Can't say I'd like it much, myself. The very idea gives me the willies, getting messages from the dead—and I'm not impressionable, like Angie Robinson seems to have been. Sounds dangerous rather than silly, when it comes to predicting someone's death. That was what happened, wasn't it? The spirits, Dido or Elissa or whoever, predicting a death?'

'That was just Felix, larking around,' she said shortly, 'pushing the glass so that it went where he wanted it to, just for fun.'

'He must've had a peculiar sense of humour, this Felix,' Mayo said mildly. Then, so sharp she almost jumped, 'Felix who?'

'Darbell. Felix Darbell.'

'Tell me about Felix Darbell.'

She stared at him, her colour a little high. 'I can only tell you what I knew then. I believe his parents were friends of Kitty and their marriage had just broken up. He was staying at Flowerdew for the summer until he went up to university. He used to help in the garden and round the house.'

'What sort of person was he? Likeable? Quick-tempered, maybe?'

'He was only a boy.' She shrugged, avoiding a direct

answer. 'About twenty, and you know how young people can fly off the handle, how impatient they can be. It sometimes makes them appear arrogant—especially when they're clever, like Felix was. He could give the impression of being rather supercilious at times.'

'And who else was there?'

'I'm not sure if I can remember.'

'Well, you must have been, for one. And Angie. Presumably Mrs Lawrence—'

'Yes, Sophie was there,' she said levelly.

Her performance so far was as well-rehearsed as Sophie Lawrence's. The two of them had spoken, he was sure. He wondered how close their relationship was.

'Oh, we keep in touch,' she answered when he asked.

'And Felix Darbell was also there that night? Mrs Wilbraham, for another, perhaps?'

'No, Kitty had gone to bed.'

'What happened, Dr Freeman? What happened that preyed on Angie Robinson's mind all this time?'

She was wearing her engagement ring this morning, an elaborate cluster of emeralds and diamonds set in dull gold that looked well on her strong, capable hands. She moved the ring round and round as she spoke, in an unconscious gesture that reminded him of Sophie Lawrence twisting her bracelets. 'As far as I can remember, Angie made no objection at first. It wasn't until the glass started whizzing round and spelling out "Dido"—only because Felix was pushing it, I'm sure!—that she started getting frightened.'

'Why?'

'Why was she frightened? Well, Dido, which you perhaps don't know, was the name of a queen of ancient Carthage. Angie hated all that stuff about the past, especially when Kitty would begin to reminisce about her work on the ruins in Carthage. She and her husband, Alfred Wilbraham, were quite famous for the work they did there. Kitty had had an extension built on to the house as a study, and it was

full of rather sinister mementoes they'd brought home—
like a mask of the goddess Tanit above her desk. She used
to relish telling the most lurid, blood-curdling stories about
children being sacrificed and thrown to the flames, that
sort of thing. She was one of those people with a natural
gift for story-telling, so that it all seemed to have happened
yesterday instead of three thousand years ago . . . It was
basically very interesting and informative, but Angie
couldn't stand it. She always shut her ears to anything
unpalatable.' The doctor sighed. 'But Felix was really very
naughty. He knew what a phobia she had and I'm afraid
he was playing her up that night. Angie realized this when
the glass spelled out "Dido" and, as far as I remember, it
was after that it all ended in confusion, the table got tipped
up and the glass broke and that was the end of it.'

'You mean there was a quarrel?'

'Not really. It just wasn't a very pleasant end to the
evening. I suppose tempers were a bit frayed, but what I
can't see is how it could possibly have anything to do with
Angie—well, with the way she died. Didn't she say, in that
letter? Could I see it?'

'I'd sooner you didn't. But I can tell you that the implication was that someone was murdered that night. And we
believe that's why she herself was killed.'

'Another murder—that night? Surely you don't believe
that?'

'Unfortunately, it seems only too likely. And that it was
Mrs Wilbraham.'

'But I've told you, Kitty was in bed. That's ridiculous!'

Mayo let her struggle with the question of whether or
not to speak. 'You asked me before what Angie was like,'
she said at last. 'I couldn't tell you then, it was too soon
after . . . too painful, but if I'm honest, I have to say she'd
do anything for attention. Believe me, Mr Mayo, nobody
was murdered that night. If Angie pretended that, she was

just drawing attention to herself, to make people feel sorry for her. She couldn't help it.'

'That's always a possibility, I suppose. But don't forget, Miss Robinson herself has been murdered—and after she'd sent that letter to us. If it wasn't that she was prepared to talk about what she knew, can you suggest any other reason why she was killed?'

It took her some time to answer. 'You have to understand she was a woman with a huge persecution complex—a chip on the shoulder. She believed people avoided her because her face was marked, ugly. She blamed that for not being liked, poor Angie, when really . . . I'm afraid she could be spiteful, and that could have upset quite a few people.'

'Enough to murder her?'

'Who knows?'

He prepared to leave, capping his pen, sliding his notebook into his inside pocket. 'I'll bear in mind what you've said, Dr Freeman. Meanwhile, have you any idea how we could get in touch with Mr Darbell?'

'With Felix? No, I'm sorry. I haven't seen him from that time to this.'

'What university was he going to?'

She shook her head. 'One of the Redbricks, I think . . .'

'Never mind, we'll find him. Oh, and there's just one more thing. I'm sure you've seen this before.' His hand came from his pocket with the earring held out on his palm.

She went very white. 'It's Angie's, of course. Where— did you get it?'

'It was found in her car.'

'Oh. Oh, I see.'

They were hook-in type earrings with a fine wire which passed through the pierced earlobe, and in the struggle to get her into the car it was not impossible this one had become dislodged and fallen into the side pocket on the passenger side, where it had been found. But nobody had yet figured out how the tiny piece of black polythene—

quite possibly a fragment pulled from a dustbin liner, which had been caught on the base of the hook itself—had got there. It wasn't much to go on, and damn-all else had been found inside the car, except traces of Angie herself: fingerprints, and several of her blonde hairs on the back of the driving seat where they might have expected to be found —but also on the passenger seat, confirming the theory that she had been propped up there after she was killed, before being driven up to Hartopp Moor. Traces of the peaty moorland soil had been found adhering to the underside of the white Astra.

'They're old, aren't they? And valuable?' He knew now that the metal was pure silver, set with semi-precious carnelian and turquoise.

'More from sentiment's sake. Kitty gave them to her.'

He left the surgery, not wholly satisfied with the interview but not entirely displeased, either, though viewing much of what the doctor had said about that night fourteen years ago with some scepticism. He'd advanced one step further than he had with Sophie Lawrence, though, in that he had an admission that something, even if it was only an innocent game of table-tapping, had occurred. But innocence was not part of this equation, of that he was sure. He was convinced now that Angie Robinson's letter, however misguided or embroidered with her own fantasies, or even if it had simply been written out of spite against Felix Darbell for winding her up, had basically given a true picture of what had happened. It made sense now to believe that it was Kitty Wilbraham's murder that night which had eventually led to the finding of Angie's body on Hartopp Moor.

Back at the station, he found Dexter's report on the Bulstrode Street flat on his desk. The SOCO sergeant had confirmed Mayo's suspicions, stating that in his opinion no struggle had taken place there; neither had the packing cases revealed anything that could help with the inquiry. The team had by now also been along to Kilbracken Road and looked at Angie Robinson's former room there, but she had left it stripped bare to the old-fashioned bedroom suite, the carpet and the curtains and nothing suspicious had been found. It was Dexter's considered opinion that Angie Robinson had met her death in neither place.

On the plus side, however, the latent prints which had been lifted from the whisky bottle and the glass in the flat had proved not to be the victim's. Identical ones had also been found on the doorknob. The glass had been subjected to saliva tests and the prints had been computer-checked but did not match the records of any known criminal. So, if the man who had visited her the night she died and made free of her whisky had been this man Felix Darbell, he did not have a criminal record.

In fact, most of their findings so far seemed to have been of a negative nature. None of the house agents in the town had had any dealings with the victim, the house-to-house team had drawn a blank in finding anyone who had known her in any intimate capacity. She had never made any close friends among her colleagues at the hospital; outside working hours, she had mixed only with the other women working for the hospital campaign—and had known them only on that basis, seeing them on the three nights a week when they had assembled to run the campaign at the old chapel, but not at other times. She hadn't been popular but nobody had been close enough to her for her to have aroused any emotion in them stronger than a vague dislike. Certainly nothing which could have induced in them any murderous intent. Outwardly, a piteously bleak and barren life, with no hint of what lay churning beneath the surface.

'What's up? You're looking chuffed,' Kite remarked to Abigail as she came to perch on the edge of his desk, watching him pecking away with two fingers at the typewriter.

She was feeling cheerful, if the truth be told. She'd been hoping fiercely to be allowed to remain as Mayo's dedicated sergeant but had realistically accepted that he wasn't going to make do with second best any longer than he had to. He and Martin Kite were a good team, who complemented each other and were used to working together. As soon as he could, he'd have Kite working with him again. It wasn't a personal matter, it was common sense.

But Kite was stuck with the child pornography case; nobody was willing to risk screwing up an inquiry that had taken three months to bring to fruition by not getting it right in the last stages. This was the boring part, difficult for anybody but especially for one of Kite's gung-ho temperament. He was still up to his ears in interviewing witnesses, his natural inclinations being to pull out all the stops and go for the bastards, but following instructions to handle it with kid gloves since two of the men were local big wheels and however it was dealt with, it was going to cause a stink.

'It's beginning to look as though we have a suspect, Martin.'

'This Darbell, is it?' He sat back and reached for yet another mug of coffee, making a face when he found it empty.

'He was in all the right places, including the night of that first putative murder in 1979, at Flowerdew. Apparently there was only one man present that night, so in that case Darbell must be the "he" who failed to keep his temper —which figures. He seems to have had a fairly low flashpoint.'

Suddenly, she gave a toss to her thick plait, threw a radiant smile at Kite and said, 'Chuck that report over, Martin, and I'll type it for you if you'll go down and fetch me some coffee. I can't bear to see anyone making such a hamfisted job. I've got half an hour before the gaffer wants me.'

She'd told herself she'd had her moment in the sun and it was now back to her cake and milk. But now—glory! A few minutes ago, Mayo had told her he wanted her to remain on the case and added, 'High time we went to have a look at this place, Flowerdew. I don't suppose there's much to be gained from an empty house but it's beginning to intrigue me the way it keeps cropping up. Time for us to take a shufty at it.'

CHAPTER 13

It was hard to imagine the scene as he'd last seen it: the rain lashing down on to the dark moorland, the pathetic body of Angie Robinson lying beneath the plastic shelter. The truck-driver McKinley's alibi had been confirmed: at nine o'clock, two hours' journey away, he had apparently been eating egg and chips in a motorway café in company with several other drivers who were prepared to confirm this. He would no doubt be relieved to know that Mayo had mentally crossed him off his list of suspects and was looking nearer home.

Hartopp Moor took on a totally different aspect in the daylight. Bare and windswept today, it had its own peculiar beauty, a wild emptiness, with the odd clump of yellow furze and the young heather, not yet in bloom, bending to a scouring wind. A bright sun reflected the occasional black, oily gleam beneath the sedge, indicating peat beneath. Mayo, who had been born within a few miles of the Brontë Parsonage and missed its bracing ambience, wound down his window to let the clean, cold air rush in, while Abigail did her best not to flinch. The cry of a curlew was the only sound. There was an empty, unimpeded view for miles.

'Next left, I think, Abigail.'

Almost at once the turning materialized, a narrow road

which dropped into what might have been a different world, so different was it from the moor they'd been crossing.

The Morwen valley was pretty, soft and fertile even at this season when the trees and hedgerows were bare, but with the occasional field of winter wheat already showing pale spears, the quickthorn greening over and wild cherry showing pale stars of blossom. Now and again, signs of habitation appeared: a farm or two, a grey church and a cluster of cottages.

The road meandered unhurriedly through the valley until eventually, three or four miles past the church and the last of the cottages, they came to the place they were looking for. It was situated in a hollow, a decaying tree-girt house built of rosy Elizabethan brick, gabled and timbered, with a sagging roof and tall, twisted chimneys. Smaller than Mayo had expected, though small in this sense was relative: compared with your average three- or four-bedroomed semi it was pretty big, though not by any means a mansion. Surrounded by a high brick wall, only the roofs and upper storeys were clearly visible from the road.

Abigail cut the engine and went to try the pair of high, rusty, wrought-iron gates which proved, not unexpectedly, to be locked. She looked round and saw that on the other side of the road a grassy knoll rose directly opposite the house. Scaling it nimbly, she made room for Mayo to scramble up beside her. From their new vantage-point they were able to see right over the wall and observe the tranquil scene spread out before them.

The deserted house looked peaceful and undisturbed, as though it felt it had existed long enough and was now, without regret, slowly crumbling into the earth. Reflected in the still waters of the lake which stretched in front of it, it had stood like this for centuries, a jewel of a house, true to the original conception of its builder. Until some twentieth-century vandal had added the absurd, minaret-like structure which was tacked on to one end—stuccoed,

domed and once painted blue and white. This was no doubt
Kitty Wilbraham's doing, the study she had added on to
house the gruesome mementoes of her working life. 'How's
that for an improvement on the scenery?' Abigail asked,
making a face.

Mayo grunted. He thought it the sort of outrage local
planning authorities ought not to allow people to get away
with, though more than likely permission hadn't even been
asked, with the relative isolation of the house giving Kitty
Wilbraham cause to feel she could cock a snook at authority, that what she did with her own property was nobody
else's business.

'Might be an idea to take a gander round the back,'
he said, curious to know more of this house where Kitty
Wilbraham had lived.

Behind the house rose an extensive belt of woodland,
stretching out to the left, while most of the foreground was
taken up by the tadpole-shaped lake which appeared to run
out at its narrow end towards a boathouse in the distance
and thence to join the river, a glimpse of which could just
be seen beyond the trees. A wall surrounded the property
and like the house it was crumbling and decaying, over-
grown with ivy and toadflax and following the road at least
as far as the next bend. A speculative look appeared in
Mayo's eye and Abigail had a nasty premonition she was
going to be instructed to scale the damn thing.

'Looks as if it's held up only by hope and the grace of
God,' she offered hopefully.

Mayo, however, was slithering down the bank and taking
his boots from the back of the car. 'We'll follow it round.
There'll be some way in at the back or I'm a Chinaman.'

He set off at a fast pace and now knowing by repute the
alacrity with which the gaffer welcomed the chance of a
walk, preferably on the rougher mountains of Wales, or the
remoter Scottish moors, and the longer the better, plus her
own antipathy to walking anywhere but on the paved

streets of a town or city, Abigail groaned, tucked her trousers into her boots, then set off at a canter to catch up with Mayo's long strides.

About a hundred yards further along, just after the sharp bend in the road, the wall turned at right angles to the hedgerow, continuing upwards along the edge of a ploughed field. They first had to push through the scrubby hedge of hawthorn, beech and field maple, then walk along the margin of the field whose deeply ridged furrows followed the line of the wall, here in a considerably worse state of repair than along the front, with gaps in it like a boxer's front teeth. Another fifty yards and the wall petered out altogether and the woodland began, a mixed plantation of coniferous and deciduous trees.

Leading between the trees was a path running parallel with the house, thick with the mast of beech and oak, springy with pine needles that deadened their footsteps. It was dark beneath the canopy but lit here and there by the brassy, hopeful gleam of aconites alongside the bramble-snagged and obviously little-used path. It wasn't until the house eventually came into sight, slightly below where they stood, that they paused to take stock. The silence was total, apart from the croo-croo of the wood pigeons and the stirring of the small wind in the bare branches above.

Then, ripping the silence apart, came the slam of a shotgun. Pellets sang past their ears and bit into the trunk of a spruce, chips of soft bark flew as the sound ricocheted through the clearing. The two detectives covered a lot of space in a very short time and froze, flattening themselves behind tree-trunks. Outraged pigeons clattered up into the trees before the woods settled again into silence.

'What are you doing here? Don't you know this is private property?'

A cautious look showed a man standing watching them with a gun to his shoulder, a dark-browed individual with a closed expression and a black labrador at his heels.

'We're police officers and what the hell d'you think you're doing with that gun?' Mayo demanded, emerging from the shelter of his tree.

'Rabbiting. Think yourselves lucky you didn't get hurt. I didn't see you there.'

This was a patent lie. They had been standing in plain view in the middle of the clearing and the gun had without doubt been aimed deliberately. Aimed to miss, maybe, to put the fear of God into them, but aimed, all the same.

'You own this property?'

'I keep an eye on the house here, look after the grounds. I've a smallholding over there.' The man jerked his head backwards.

'In that case you can give us a few minutes of your time.'

He debated this. Then he gave a brusque nod and said grudgingly that they'd better come over to his cottage, whistled for the dog and began to walk away, leaving them to follow him across the top edge of the ploughed field and into a small cleanly-swept farmyard surrounding a tiny, brick-built cottage with a slate roof. The yard had a tidy air of self-sufficiency, despite a clapped-out old motorbike standing in one corner and a pigsty in the other. As they walked towards the cottage a big shire horse gave a loud whinny and thrust a gentle, inquiring head over the door of a stable nearly the size of the cottage itself.

'No need for that,' Abigail was told as she tried to knock off the earth clinging to her boots at the doorstep, 'I'm not houseproud.' She took them off, all the same, leaving them by the door before following him into a living-room warm from an open fire in the range and redolent with the savoury aroma of a slow-cooking stew in the fireside oven.

Plainly whitewashed, as neat and clean as the deck of a ship, the interior gave the lie to his remark. It spoke of an owner with few material needs, living alone and content to do so. A sink under the window, a scrubbed pine table in the centre, on it an old portable typewriter, a pile of paper and a ledger or two. Open plank shelves filled to capacity with books, both paperback and hardcover, ran across one wall.

'All right. Maybe you'll tell me what this is all about? Sit down.' Apart from a sagging easy chair in front of the range, there were no seats other than two wooden stools which he pulled out from under the table. Visitors were patently not encouraged. He himself ignored the easy chair. With a curt 'Basket, Nell,' to the dog, he stood with his back to the fire, facing the room. 'Well?'

Abigail availed herself of one of the two stools, but Mayo, not intending to leave the dominant position to the man he was about to question, leaned back against the sink and folded his arms. 'I'm Detective Chief Inspector Mayo and this is Sergeant Moon. And your name?'

'You can call me Tommo, everyone does.'

'Your proper name, please.'

'Maryan Thomas, spelt with a "y". You can see why I prefer Tommo.'

Mayo frowned. He had come across the name, as a man's name, before, though he couldn't immediately remember where. 'How long have you lived here, Mr Thomas?' He was damned if he was going to use the nickname, which he found ridiculous, besides being unwilling to introduce any sort of familiarity into the interview.

'Seventeen years.'

'And before that?'

The stillness before he answered was scarcely the space between one tick of the clock and the next, but this was clearly a question that wasn't welcome. At last he replied that he'd been teaching at an agricultural college in the north of England but had given it up in order to farm.

'Do you own this place?'

'I do now. It was a hovel and I lived in it rent-free when I first came here, in return for the work I put in on the house and garden.' An obvious pride lifted the heaviness of his features, and made him more loquacious. 'They call it organic farming now but for me I'd no choice if I wanted to survive. I couldn't afford fancy gadgets and expensive chemicals. I built up my smallholding, bit by bit, and in the end I was able to buy it from Kitty—from Mrs Wilbraham, the owner. She wasn't demanding in what she asked, it didn't break me,' he added ironically.

He was a taut, compactly-built individual, sturdy but with no spare fat, nothing at all extraneous about him, in fact. His answers were punctuated by considered silences. He was the sort who'd keep secrets just for the hell of it— and would be a reluctant, even downright hostile, witness. There could be violence just beneath the surface.

'Do you know a woman called Angie Robinson?'

He thought, and said eventually, 'I *did*.'

'What do you mean, did?' Mayo asked. 'How d'you know she was dead?'

That called for another pause. 'I didn't, and I hardly knew her, but I'm sorry to hear it.'

'How did you come to know her?'

'Oh, she visited the big house a few times, years ago, with Madeleine Freeman, Mrs Wilbraham's doctor. Why? Was there something suspicious about her death?'

'What makes you ask that?'

Thomas shrugged. 'Busy police . . . I hardly think you'd be here talking to me if it wasn't something like that.'

'She was murdered,' Mayo said.

Thomas received the news with another of his unreadable silences before eventually saying, 'Well, she was all sorts of a fool, Angie, but she didn't deserve that. And you're on the wrong tack if you think I'd anything to do with it.'

'Don't put words into my mouth, Mr Thomas. When was the last time you saw her?'

'Good God, you expect me to remember that? At least twelve or thirteen years ago, I'd say, maybe more. Before

Kitty went away at any rate.' But something different had entered into his tone, something guarded.

Abigail said, 'If you knew Angie Robinson, I assume you had social connections with Mrs Wilbraham, as well as working for her?'

Thomas looked at her, took in the coppery hair, the slim, neat figure and long legs, her feet curled around the bottom rail of the stool. He smiled. He had very white, even teeth. His face was very brown and weatherbeaten.

'Practically every day. Occasionally, I was even invited to dine. I do know which knife and fork to use, you know.'

Abigail flushed slightly and a dangerous spark of green lit her hazel eyes. Mayo thought: If that was bait it wasn't worth rising to. There was nothing uncouth about Thomas or his surroundings, nothing uneducated about his speech. He had no doubt the man's beginnings had been very different from the way he lived now, and if necessary these would be gone into, but, for the present, if he chose to live in circumstances likely to be regarded as primitive by the rest of society, that was his business.

'Then you'd know most of Mrs Wilbraham's friends,' Abigail said crisply, 'at any rate, those who might have known Angie Robinson. Sophie Lawrence, for instance?'

'Yes.'

'You still keep in contact?'

'Occasionally.'

'You met on Thursday in Oundle's Bookshop, in fact?'

'We did?'

'Come on, Mr Thomas, I saw you there.'

He shrugged. 'Then there's no point in denying it.'

'And you still say you hadn't heard of Angie Robinson's death until now?'

'When Sophie and I meet,' he said, 'we have other things to discuss.'

Mayo raised a figurative eyebrow at this information, which Abigail had had no opportunity of passing on since recognizing Thomas when he had first appeared in the clearing. If correct, it reinforced the impression he was getting—that the group surrounding the late Mrs Wilbraham had been a tightly integrated one, and that they were now closing ranks. Moreover, it was a group growing in number: Sophie Lawrence, Madeleine Freeman, Angie Robinson, the boy, Felix—and now this man, whom both women had omitted to say they knew, for whatever reason, or to mention as part of the Flowerdew scene. Another man who, he thought, might fit the bill, the 'he' in Angie Robinson's letter.

Abigail was pressing on and Thomas admitted he had been in Lavenstock on Thursday, but only to order farm supplies, pick up some necessary shopping and slip into Oundle's to meet Sophie. 'Any reason why I shouldn't? We meet quite often, Sophie and I, when she's in England.'

'No reason at all, Mr Thomas,' Abigail replied, and went on immediately to ask about his movements on the Tuesday night. He admitted to having no alibi, had been working outside all day and got soaked to the skin so, with the light giving out early, he'd come indoors and had a hot bath.

'Which is no easy undertaking in a place like this!' The sudden, white-toothed smile crossed his face as he indicated a wooden working surface with a curtain slung underneath, behind which presumably lurked some sort of bathing arrangements. 'Even though the range gives me plenty of hot water.' After he'd bathed and had his supper, he'd gone early to bed, like the farmer he was. He denied knowing anything at all about Bulstrode Street—and unless he had borrowed or hired a Jaguar it was unlikely he'd been the man who had apparently visited Sophie Lawrence. He didn't possess a car at all. He used his motorcycle when it was in a good mood, otherwise the thrice-weekly country bus.

'All right,' Mayo said, 'I'm sure we shall be able to check whatever's necessary. Let's get on to something else. Do you remember a young man, name of Darbell, Felix Darbell?'

'Of course. He was a student who hung around here one summer, used to give me a hand with the garden. Good worker. Why do you want to know? He wasn't particularly friendly with Angie.'

'Do you know where Mr Darbell is now?'

'Good Lord, no! Why should I?'

Again Mayo felt a pricking in his thumbs. 'It was an odd set-up here, wasn't it, an old woman like Mrs Wilbraham, and all those young people?'

'I don't see anything peculiar about that—she was always one to have young folks around her.'

'Well, maybe she felt like that, but what about the rest of you? Didn't you ever get bored? It's very quiet out here —nothing much to do of an evening—very tempting to try and liven things up with, say, a bit of fortune-telling, table-tapping or whatever—join in those seances, did you?'

'Seances? Me?' Thomas laughed shortly. He looked at Mayo with patent scorn. 'Do I strike you as the sort to go in for that sort of rubbish?'

No, thought Mayo, sensing the hostility building up once more, but he did strike him as being nifty enough to sidestep the truth when it suited him. Nevertheless, the time had come to call a halt. He knew when he'd got as much as he was likely to get from a witness for the time being. He remarked, on the point of leaving, not really expecting to gain anything fresh from the answer, 'Presumably you're paid for looking after the house and grounds, Mr Thomas? Through Mrs Wilbraham's lawyer?'

'Through her lawyer? Well, I don't see what damn business it is of yours, but no, Kitty pays me herself. She's not ga-ga yet.'

With a feeling that something solid had given way beneath him—*bloody hell!*—Mayo stuck his hands in his pockets and leaned further back against the sink. 'What do you mean by that? She sends you the money?'

'Sends it? Why the devil should she? No, I go and touch my forelock and she gives me a cheque.'

Abigail said carefully, 'We were told she'd gone to live in Tunisia.'

'So she did.' Mayo was aware of Thomas's cool, amused appraisal of the young woman. 'And came back about three months ago.'

'Where is she living?'

'At Flowerdew. Where else?'

'In that case,' Mayo said, 'we'd better get ourselves over there and start asking her some questions.'

Thomas gave a laugh, and this time it was one of pure pleasure. 'Go by all means, but she won't see you. She doesn't see anyone. She lives alone with Jessie Crowther, her housekeeper, and if you can get past her, you're a better man than I am. And if you do manage it, don't rely on what she tells you. Half the time she's OK but the other half she doesn't know the time of day.'

CHAPTER 14

Trudging back along the edge of the field towards the big house, they walked in silence, trying to digest the implications of what they had just learned.

The news that Kitty Wilbraham was still alive had knocked Mayo temporarily off-balance. He should not have assumed she was dead so easily, though granted, everything had pointed to it. But he had become so accustomed to thinking her dead and that her death constituted the motive for Angie Robinson's murder that he was having trouble adjusting his thoughts, and his only answer when Abigail spoke to him was an abstracted grunt. Presently, it occurred to him that she had spoken. 'Sorry, what was that you said?'

'I was only saying I'd better check out with that college where he taught.'

'Thomas? Yes, do that, Abigail. See what it was that caused him to leave—or be chucked out.'

'Chucked out?' She threw him a swift look. 'What did he say to make you think that, sir? Something I missed?'

'It wasn't what he said, it's what he didn't say. He's a damned sight too cagey for my liking, and too clever by half. All right, I don't blame him, I'd do the same in his position. First principle of self-preservation: never volunteer information! But I had the feeling he was laughing up his sleeve, and that I neither like nor trust. He knows what all this is about, just as Sophie Lawrence and Dr Freeman do. They're as tight as clams, but I'll have it out of them before I'm finished, Abigail, by God I will!' He was becoming more and more sure that the three of them were involved in some sort of conspiracy of silence. More than that: they were very likely taking him for a fool, though that didn't greatly dismay him. Rather the opposite. That way one or other of them would sooner or later be bound to crack.

They very soon came to a small gate let into the wall and passed through it into a dank courtyard where the sun could rarely have penetrated. The paving stones were mossy and slippery with algæ, many of them cracked. Beyond the yard was a glimpse of disused stables and tumbledown outhouses.

They banged hard on the back door, as advised, and waited. 'Otherwise she'll never hear you, she's as deaf as a post,' Thomas had warned. 'And maybe won't answer anyway, if she doesn't choose to. They're two for a pair, Jessie and Kitty, keep themselves bolted in like two old nuns in a convent, which is just as well, considering how isolated the house is. They won't hear of having someone younger to live in and look after them. I keep a weather eye on them, though,' he added laconically, 'get their groceries in and so on.'

Jessie Crowther must have been in a good mood. They were allowed to enter after she'd examined them through the kitchen window, heard them yell who they were through the letter-box and been told three times that Tommo had sent them. Minutes later, the door opened with a grinding of bolts, after which the old woman led them along a dark passageway, through a gloomy scullery and finally into an equally gloomy kitchen. But, having let them in, she resolutely refused to allow them to see Mrs Wilbraham. A crafty look crossed the weathered old face when she heard their request. 'She's too old to be bothered with all that,' she said evasively. Jessie herself must have been in her early seventies if she was a day. 'What's he sent you here for then—Tommo?'

The question was clearly a matter of form: there was an old black telephone on a shelf in the corner and Thomas, for all his alternative lifestyle, had possessed one, too.

'Perhaps you'd better sit down, Miss Crowther,' Mayo suggested. 'This may take a bit of time.'

'*Mrs* Crowther,' she corrected sharply. A little round body of a northcountrywoman, there appeared to be little wrong with her physically, apart from her deafness, which didn't seem to bother her unduly, now that she could watch their lips move with her sharp, bright-eyed stare.

'Sit yourselves down, then. You'll join me in my elevenses,' she announced, in a tone brooking no argument. Waving them to seats at the table, she filled the electric kettle at a huge ceramic sink, chipped and stained with age and use, busying herself at the cupboards and presently slapping down on to the table three mugfuls of hot chocolate and three plates, each containing an awesome-sized piece of Yorkshire parkin.

The kitchen was a cavernous place where enormous cupboards and a bulbous fridge of ancient vintage loomed, with dark corners where the heat from the Aga could never conceivably reach. And that was the reason, Mayo

assumed, for the cosy corner which had been arranged as
near as possible to the stove and the black iron fireplace,
having on its hearth a two-bar electric fire. On a faded rug
in front of it stood a couple of basket chairs, one occupied
by a red cushion, a piece of knitting and a tortoiseshell cat.
Most likely the rest of the house was shut off and unused.
It smelt overpoweringly of damp, and perhaps mice. No
wonder the cat looked so satisfied. Mayo looked specula-
tively at the second chair, wondering how much time the
other occupant of the house spent here, if any—or whether,
considering her great age, she spent most of her time in
bed. Or even (which did not seem so improbable) if she
were simply a ghost in everyone's mind.

'Help yourselves.' Jessie Crowther sat herself down,
waved to their plates. The unasked-for chocolate and sweet-
stuff at this time in the morning was a novelty Mayo wasn't
sure he wanted but he followed Abigail's example and got
on with it, finding the hot drink surprisingly welcome. And
was able to say with authority that the parkin was genuine:
crunchy with oatmeal, sweet with black treacle and spicy
with ginger.

'Things you hear about nowadays!' Mrs Crowther commented when she heard what they had to tell about Angie
Robinson. 'You never think it'll happen to somebody you
know.'

'I'm sorry we've had to bring you such bad news.'

'Oh well, as to that, can't say as I knew her enough to
be upset . . . All right, is it?' she asked Abigail, who had a
hearty appetite but was finding some difficulty in disposing
of such a substantial portion.

'Very tasty, Mrs Crowther. Lovely.'

'Like another piece? You look as though you could do
with feeding up—you young women, thin as a match with
the wood scraped off, and still not content!'

Regretfully, Abigail smiled and shook her head, swallowed the last of the crumbs and slid her hand inside her

shoulder-bag for her pocketbook. 'Delicious, but I couldn't eat another morsel.'

'Suit yourself, I know somebody who'll finish it up. Always had a sweet tooth and very partial to my parkin, she is.'

Mayo brought the conversation back to where they'd left off. 'Did Miss Robinson visit here often, Mrs Crowther?'

'I wouldn't say that, just sometimes, with the doctor. Even though Kitty didn't really care for her. Couldn't be doing with her myself. She must've been thick-skinned, for she used to come, all the same, invited or not, and Kitty would never turn anybody away. Liberty Hall here it was, in them days.' There was going to be no stopping her, once her memories had been released. 'Oh, Flowerdew was different then,' she went on, 'you should've seen it— should've seen Kitty! She was old then, mind, but lively. It set her up, having all them youngsters around her. It's never having had children of her own, I reckon.'

'Can you remember the exact date when Mrs Wilbraham went back to Tunisia?' Mayo asked. 'And why d'you think she did?'

There was a pause while Mrs Crowther did some calculating. '1979. Middle of August,' she said eventually. 'And why? I don't know, but I expect she felt she'd been away too long. It had a kind of pull, d'you see? That was her life, really, it was what she loved, what'd made her and her husband famous. I do know she had some daft idea about being near him, she's never really got over him dying out there. It's forever Alfred this, Alfred that.'

'What brought her back here, then?'

'Better medical care, for one thing, her arthritis gets no better. I was glad to get back here, I can tell you! I used to wonder sometimes what we were doing out there. Too hot for one thing, and all that funny food—and the flies!'

'Nowhere like home, is there, Mrs Crowther? But before you went away . . . was there anyone else besides yourself and Mrs Wilbraham living in the house? Can you remember?'

''Course I can. Nothing wrong with my memory when it comes to folks—and there's been some right funniosities here from time to time, I can tell you!' Giving him a sideways glance, she added, 'That Irena, for one.'

'Irena? Who was she?'

'Bron, that was her name, Irena Bron. Czech, she was. I'd have checked her!' She chuckled grimly at what was obviously an old joke. 'Moody. And talk about a temper! Once threw a box of eggs from one end of my kitchen to t'other. Something I'd said upset her, about them nasty foreign sausages she used to cook, and dumplings I'd have been ashamed to give to the cat!'

Irena Bron. Yet another name to add to the growing list. Another who had been present that night when the spirits were conjured up? 'Tell me what you knew about her, Mrs Crowther, about Irena Bron,' Mayo asked, and knew it was a question she'd been waiting for by the readiness of her answer.

'Well, she wasn't as young as the rest of them, that's for sure. She'd never see thirty-five again, nearer forty, if you ask me. Dark, had a moustache. Some of these foreign women do, you know. Her father had worked before the war with Kitty and Dr Wilbraham—he was Kitty's husband that died—and when *he* died, this Bron chap, Irena came here and Kitty took her in out of the goodness of her heart. Wished she hadn't many a time, I dare say, for she was nothing but trouble, what with that nasty temper of hers and all.'

'What happened to her?'

'Went to work down south and good riddance!'

'When did she leave?'

But at this point Mrs Crowther's deafness suddenly began to trouble her again. She didn't answer, busy gathering together the plates and mugs.

The light was switched on in the kitchen, though the central pendant with its single harsh bulb didn't achieve much in the way of illumination, except to throw the old woman's face into shadow as she moved from table to sink. Mayo thought she was older even than he'd thought, possibly nearer eighty than seventy, and he felt a reluctance to press her to remember things possibly painful to her. Then she turned round and smiled, and he knew that, in a way, she was welcoming his questions. Indeed, he was ready to hazard a guess that Jessie had probably never known for sure exactly what had happened, though maybe she had suspected, and would dearly like to have her suspicions confirmed now and her curiosity at last satisfied.

'Who else used to visit about that time?' asked Abigail, pencil poised above the still almost blank page.

There'd been Sophie Amhurst, who came every day to work for Kitty, and Dr Freeman, who came three times a week regular as clockwork, and sometimes more on a social visit, bringing Angie, her shadow, with her. And that young lad that lived here for a while. Felix whatsisname?'

'Darbell?'

'That's it! Can't tell you much about him, mind. You want to ask Tommo, he used to help him in the garden.' Her face softened as she spoke the man's name. 'Tommo would know more about him.'

I'm damn sure he would, thought Mayo. And about Irena Bron. But whether he'd tell what he knew was another matter. He pushed his chair back and stood up. 'Thanks for the hot chocolate, Mrs Crowther, very welcome, and the parkin. It's a long time since I had any as good as that. You've as light a hand at baking as my mother, and that's saying something.'

The old woman was delighted. 'Bless you, I could make it with my eyes shut! Would you like the recipe? It's no trouble.' Reluctant to admit them at first, she was now unwilling to let go of her unexpected visitors.

'Save it for the next time we come, Mrs Crowther, I'd be delighted to have it,' Abigail replied, earning herself a beaming smile. Seemingly, Jessie accepted that there would be a next time without the idea bothering her.

'You can go out by the front door,' she said, when at last she ran out of excuses to detain them. 'Save you going all the way round the back. I'll come down to the gate with you and open it.'

Donning a large woven cloak-like garment reminiscent of a Berber rug, she hooked down a key from behind the door and motioned them to follow.

A baize-lined door with the baize hanging off it led at the end of a corridor into the hall, panelled in time-darkened oak, with a magnificent, though badly flaking, plaster ceiling. A wide, dog-leg staircase with carved newel-posts led upwards into impenetrable shadow. On the staircase walls gloomy ancestors gave each other unfriendly stares. The fungoid smell was even more pervasive here, with even stronger overtones of mice. A slight film of moisture overlaid the flagstones: there was unlikely to be a damp course and the deep wainscots were probably full of wet or dry rot. It was dismayingly cold.

All the charm of this house, Mayo decided as they came thankfully out into the clean, cold air, resided in its exterior.

As Jessie Crowther pulled the heavy door to behind them, Mayo stood looking at the lake. With its sapling-crowned island in the centre, banked by willows now dipping golden wands to the water, it ran almost up to the foundations of the house, with only a narrow flagged path separating the two. It was full of rank weeds, muddy and swollen, no doubt, from the recent heavy rains. The old boathouse at the far end seemed to be in total disrepair.

He remarked on the stuccoed extension tacked on to the end of the house, inquiring as to its function.

'Oh, that's just Kitty's old workroom, full of old junk.'

Mrs Crowther pulled her cloak closer round her and toddled off down the drive at a brisk pace, leaving them to follow.

'I've just thought on,' she said unexpectedly after she had unlocked the almost seized-up iron gates, allowing them to be pushed open enough to squeeze through. 'It's always been in my mind how funny it was, the way Kitty upped and left here, just as soon as she'd got rid of that Irena. You'd have thought she'd have been thankful to stay here nice and quiet without her, wouldn't you? But no, the day after she'd gone she says to me, "Jessie, it's time to go back," and within a week there we were in Tunis.' Her bright eyes were fixed unwaveringly on Mayo's face as she spoke. 'Come again, when I've had time for another think. I might have remembered a bit more.'

What she remembered would depend on Kitty, her mistress, that was what she meant.

And Mayo said sternly that yes, they'd be back.

And what *he* meant was that it wouldn't be long before they were, and the next time it would be Kitty Wilbraham they'd see. He was beginning to feel that only then would he be able to accept the fact that she really was alive. Only this time, he'd come with another murder victim in mind. For if Kitty Wilbraham hadn't been killed, who had, other than Irena Bron? Unless they happened to discover that she too, like Kitty, was still alive.

'It would fit,' Abigail said, 'depending on how you read the last part of that letter. "*She would not have died if she had stayed away from England*" doesn't necessarily mean if Mrs Wilbraham had stayed in Tunisia. It could mean if Irena Bron had never left Czechoslovakia.'

'It could,' said Mayo.

CHAPTER 15

'I don't mind having lies told to me, Abigail—well, not much, it's what I expect—but what I do object to is when they expect me to believe 'em.'

Abigail made sympathetic noises, though the predictability of the Great British Public's willingness to think that anyone who joined the police force was so thick they were asking to be lied to was almost monotonous.

Madeleine Freeman, when questioned again on the subject of the evening at Flowerdew, had coolly asserted that she'd completely forgotten that the woman Irena Bron had also been there the night they tried the table-tapping. She couldn't remember which firm in the City she had gone to work for.

Sophie Lawrence in her turn admitted that she hadn't wanted to talk about the evening at all, simply because it had seemed so childish and stupid in retrospect. Grownups, you know, behaving like schoolchildren.

Thomas, when pressed, also reluctantly admitted to being present, at least for part of the time. He'd walked out before they even started the bloody game, he said, and he was the only one Mayo believed to be telling the truth, on that point at any rate. As to the rest of it, he looked on the whole thing with a very jaundiced eye. 'They're all lying their heads off, for some reason I haven't yet discovered— but don't let them think they can keep that up for ever! One of them will crack, sooner or later.'

Felix Darbell? None of them admitted to knowing what Felix had been doing with the rest of his life.

And then at last Dr Freeman had found her memory sufficiently revived to recall the name of the firm that Irena Bron had gone to work for in the City—which turned out to have gone into liquidation years ago. What, he wondered, had made her change her mind? It was a question which irritated him, like a piece of grit in an oyster shell, but producing no pearls.

The job of tracing the erstwhile company secretary fell to Farrar, who was happy to throw himself into it and who soon came up with the news that the secretary was an old fellow, now retired and living with his daughter near Warwick. 'Handy,' Mayo said. 'Get yourself over there, Keith, and see what you can learn from the old chap, if he's not too far gone to remember.'

But Norman Kington was very much in the here and now. He'd taken early retirement when his firm went bust and was even now only just on seventy, a sprightly, soldierly type possessing all his faculties, including an excellent memory, a taste for malt whisky and a willingness to share it. Farrar, alarmed by the size of the first slug he poured, reluctantly declined one for himself and confined his acceptance of refreshment to a cup of coffee made by Kington's daughter, while Kington himself told him that he remembered Irena Bron very clearly: first because she'd been the best candidate by far for the job and secondly because she'd never turned up for it.

'She wrote us a letter, two days later, making apologies. Decided to go back to Czechoslovakia, so she said, and I confess I wasn't altogether sorry. Hadn't liked the look of her much at the interview, but she had damn good qualifications, better than anyone else, I'll say that for her. She made the right choice in not coming to us as it turned out—couple of years later the firm winked up.'

Farrar thanked him for his cooperation, left him to his whisky, and drove back to Lavenstock where, his mission accomplished, he was put on to what he saw as the menial task of ringing round the universities and persuading them to look up the name of Felix Darbell in their student admissions lists for 1979.

While he was still occupied with this, the object of his search was sitting in his office chair, which he had occupied without moving since his customary arrival time of eight-fifteen. A full workload was spread on the desk in front of him and he hadn't even started on it by ten, but sat unoccupied, doing nothing, staring into the distance, an unheard-of occurrence. To see a pile of papers he must get through, a list of meetings he must attend, were things which never in the normal course of events daunted or depressed Felix. It gave him a sense of importance, an identity without which he would have been nothing. His work was the only thing that had come to matter to him, that and the power it brought. Not the wealth, or the prestige, but the work itself. Not even Lorna came within miles of that sort of satisfaction. Especially not Lorna.

But this Monday morning was different from the rest. Some time during the sleepless hours of the previous night he had been forced to admit to himself that the situation had reached crunch point. It was borne in on him, more clearly than ever before, how miserably the events of fourteen years ago had blighted his life. He at last admitted that he had been reduced to an automaton, a zombie. He had lived under the shadow of those events and would do so until the day he breathed his last. Up to now, he had found it possible to live with himself by the simple expedient of believing he had expunged Kitty and all that had happened at Flowerdew from his thoughts, in the same way that Sophie vowed she had done. Unlike Sophie, he had not simply left it at that. He had a strongly self-protective streak that told him one day chickens might come home to roost and he had planned his life and his escape routes accordingly. It was the reason he lived as he did, kept his money in secret places, his affairs tied up tight as a drum,

Lorna left well-provided for. He had allowed himself to make no close friends, and was an enigma to those acquaintances he shared with Lorna.

He had never consciously admitted to having arranged his life thus deliberately, even to himself . . . but now he knew that he had done exactly that, because of the fear that had always been there, the root cause of the intermittent nightmares that woke him in a black sweat: not through guilt at what had happened, but in panic that one day it would all come to light. As it must, inexorably, now. And be worse by ten-fold than it would have been two weeks ago, before the death of Angie Robinson. It was get out and go time.

He swept the day's work together into a pile in the centre of his desk, not bothering even to read his morning's mail. From now on, all that would be someone else's pigeon—Preston's, probably, who wouldn't be able to believe his luck. Into his briefcase Felix put the few personal belongings he kept at the office—an electric razor, a clean shirt and a few spare handkerchiefs—and left.

He didn't even tell his open-mouthed secretary where he was going. He contemplated doing so, and savoured for a moment the pleasure he'd get from informing her why it was necessary, but he couldn't be bothered. He contented himself with knowing that Preston would have her out of her chair, and his own secretary in it, before the week was out.

He drove at leisurely pace through the well-heeled Surrey countryside, surprised that he felt no urgency, heading towards Guildford and the Hog's Back, to the widely-spaced estate of executive homes, excluded from public gaze by a mini-forest of pines and rhododendron. He turned into the drive of his own acre and a half, wherein reposed the new five-bedroomed Tudorbethan-style house that was Lorna's pride and joy, her reward for not making too much fuss about the non-existent children who might have occupied some of the bedrooms. He had drawn the line at that. Children created complications he could do without.

Lorna hadn't seen it that way at first. There had been tears and pleadings, a long spell on tranquillizers, but in the end he'd been able to persuade her. She stopped crying and peering into prams and her lips no longer trembled when she looked at her friends' babies. Instead, she passed most of her time with her nose buried in *Vogue* and glossy interior decorating magazines of the sort featuring other people's houses, and then spent his money endlessly on doing up their own house and on clothes and make-up and falderals for herself. She seemed happy enough, now.

He drove slowly up the curving gravel drive and when he came in sight of the house and saw the car drawn up next to Lorna's new Renault, his heart plunged and he knew this was it. With a fatalistic sense of inevitability, he realized why he'd had no sense of urgency this morning. Though he hadn't expected the game to be up quite so soon, he'd known in his heart that ultimately he wasn't going to get away with a thing. He was only mildly surprised that what he basically felt was a great upsurge of relief. He opened the car door and walked into the house to face the police.

The man standing at the bottom of the stairs was about his own age, fair-haired, red-faced, and open-mouthed. For a split second, Felix wondered why a policeman should be carrying a bottle of white wine and two glasses. Even more puzzling was why he was only half-dressed and in his stockinged feet. And why Lorna should be standing half way down the steps, wearing nothing but a sexy negligée he hadn't seen before and a look of total horror on her face.

As the truth dawned on him, all the repressions of fourteen years welled up inside him, the temper he thought he'd learned to control beat in his temples. There was a roaring in his head, and with a great bellow, he sprang forward.

The following day, sick to the back teeth of looking for dark green Jags, Pete Deeley took himself off to stretch his legs and call for a tea-break in the bus station caff. He was reading the paper, heedless of the reek of frying chips and the pungency of the gooey sauce bottle on the table in front of him, when he noticed a filler paragraph under the headline LAID BARE. What he read nearly caused him to choke on his second jam doughnut:

> Mr Felix Darbell, a company director, who on Monday morning returned home unexpectedly from his office and surprised his wife and a man in a state of undress on the staircase, was yesterday remanded on bail for attacking Mr David Fernley, a solicitor, and causing grievous bodily harm. When Mr Fernley was attacked he defended himself with a bottle of wine he happened to be holding at the time, injuring Mr Darbell. Both men had to be taken to Guildford General Hospital but were later released after treatment. 'It was a storm in a teacup,' said Mrs Lorna Darbell, thirty-three.

'I take it all back,' said Atkins avuncularly. 'I take it all back, Pete—there must be something good comes out of all that effort you put into reading the *Sun*. This is going to speed things up. Guildford, you say?' His hand reached for the telephone.

CHAPTER 16

'All the way from Leeds, Mr Darbell? You drove all the way from Leeds, made a detour via Lavenstock where you spent less than an hour with Mrs Lawrence, and then drove back to Guildford? All this to see a woman you hadn't seen

—or even been in contact with—for fourteen years? Takes some swallowing, that.'

'That isn't my problem.'

Felix Darbell, a handsome man with a high-bridged nose, fairish hair and light, cold blue eyes, looked pale and patrician as he sat in the interview room, his looks marred somewhat by the large strip of plaster over his left temple. He sat with his legs crossed and would have seemed quite composed, apart from his hands, which trembled, and his forehead, which was damp with sweat.

But he was sticking to his story, that he hadn't seen Angie Robinson for more years than he could remember, that he had never even heard of Bulstrode Street, that he'd only spent an hour or so with Sophie Lawrence. 'Which she'll confirm if you take the trouble to ask her.'

'She's not going to be much help to you. She's denied having any visitors that night.'

At that, he flushed darkly. 'She said that? Sophie? I don't believe you!'

'Yes, she did, Mr Darbell. So where were you? You've admitted you were in Lavenstock, and I suggest you were at Angie Robinson's flat in Bulstrode Street.'

'No.'

'Not a very salubrious place, Bulstrode Street—and not the sort of place to park a car like yours, either, if you don't want it noticed. It was seen, Mr Darbell. It was there from eight to eight-thirty on the night she was murdered.'

Darbell said, 'I did not kill Angie Robinson. I did not go to her flat.'

Mayo leaned back in his chair, Abigail Moon sat a little way behind him, with Farrar leaning against the wall because there wasn't room in the small space for another chair and it was his fate always to be at the end of the line.

'Well, I have irrefutable proof you did. How else do you suggest your fingerprints got there, on the doorknob, and

on a whisky bottle and a glass besides? By thought trans-
ference?'

Darbell's pale eyes flickered. 'I—' be began, then flapped
his hand. 'Oh, forget it. I've nothing to say. Nothing you're
going to believe, anyway.' He uncrossed his legs, shifted
his feet. The sweat stood out thicker on his forehead.

'I should advise you to tell the truth, in view of what's
against you, Mr Darbell. You're a violent man, for one
thing. Two days ago you attacked a man at your home.
Oh, I can understand why—I wouldn't be in a sweet temper, either, if I came home and found my wife with her
lover—'

'Leave my wife out of this! She's nothing to do with it!'

'We're talking about your attitude,' Mayo said quietly,
'and that has everything to do with it. You react violently
when something upsets you, don't you? Like you did that
night at Flowerdew, fourteen years ago.'

'Flowerdew?'

Darbell's head jerked involuntarily, the pale blue eyes
were suddenly glassy. He hadn't expected that.

'I don't remember any night at Flowerdew.' But it
sounded like the first really spontaneous thing he'd said,
an automatic, instinctive denial, a step towards panic, and
as Mayo leaned forward, elbows on the table, he seemed
to realize this. His eyes flickered towards the tape-recorder
on the table and he licked his lips again. 'May I have a
drink?'

'Certainly. Somebody fetch Mr Darbell a cup of tea,'
Mayo said, without looking round. Farrar went out.

'You say you don't remember,' Mayo went on. 'Angie
Robinson did, though. She never forgot what happened.
From that night on, she was a very frightened woman.
She'd seen murder, and it had preyed on her mind ever
since. So she decided to square her conscience and tell. But
then she was strangled—right on the same night that you
were here in Lavenstock. Something of a coincidence,

wasn't it? Shall I tell you something? I don't believe in coincidences, and what's more, I'd be very surprised if you do, either.'

There was a very long silence in the interview room which Mayo allowed to continue until Farrar came back with tea in a plastic mug which he set down on the table.

Darbell drank the tea in great gulps, then sat motionless, looking at his hands spread on the table before him as though he'd never seen them before. Finally he looked up and said, 'You're determined to get me for that woman's murder—for Angie Robinson—aren't you? I didn't do it, I swear to God I didn't do it, but if I tell you the truth, I'll be in it worse than ever.'

It was as near as dammit to an admission that he'd been lying before. 'You mean what happened at Flowerdew was worse than this?' Mayo asked.

Darbell blinked and was once again struck silent, staring at the blank wall opposite. The harsh fluorescent tube was not kind to his self-absorbed, highly-charged face. He looked like a man who was thinking fast, and one at the end of his rope.

'Tell me what you know about Irena Bron,' Mayo said quietly.

It was as if the name triggered some release in Darbell. He seemed to collapse, literally, sagging in his chair. But the instinct for self-preservation was strong; almost immediately, an expression of grasping at straws crossed his face.

'All right, I'll tell you what it is,' he said. 'I've been framed, deliberately, for Angie Robinson's murder. But what I did at Flowerdew was at least done under provocation—and there are people who are witness to that.'

Mayo felt the pressure release in him, too, as if an elastic band wound tight round his skull had suddenly snapped.

'But *you're* going to tell us about it, first, aren't you? And framed? You don't seriously expect us to believe that?'

'I tell you, I was set up for this—I walked into it, if you

like—but if I want to prove that, I've no option but to tell you the rest. I'm in a cleft stick, aren't I?'

'I shan't know until you tell me. Come on, everything you can remember. It's a long time ago, but I don't suppose you've forgotten.'

'A long time?' Darbell said bitterly. 'It seems like yesterday. Angie Robinson isn't the only one who could never forget.'

He had walked out of the drawing-room at Flowerdew after the fracas with the broken tumbler, consumed with such a rage that he couldn't trust himself to remain in the same room as that woman a moment longer. If he had been in any condition to think, he would have known it was only partly Irena herself he was angry with. Much of his fury was occasioned by Sophie: he was in love for the first time in his life, but she'd made it even plainer than usual that night that she wanted nothing to do with him. It was Tommo she was really interested in, bloody Tommo who could've had her just by lifting his little finger. Frustrated, Felix directed his barbs and his sarcasms first at Angie Robinson and then at stupid, mad, unlovely and unlovable Irena, a despicable target because she was so easy to annoy.

If she had left him alone and let him cool off, he'd told himself a thousand times since, he would have got over his annoyance with her, but when she followed him out into the hall and began clawing at his sleeve, mouthing her anger, spittle flying from her mouth, actually almost wrestling with him, he could control himself no longer. He took hold of her strong, sturdy body and began to shake and pummel it as if it were no more than a lumpy pillow on a hot, sleepless night. How his hands came to be around her throat he never knew. He wasn't even conscious of her body growing limp and the congestion of her face until he heard Madeleine Freeman's voice and saw Madeleine herself, white-faced but controlled, ordering him to fetch her medical bag from her car, quick, quick! It took him no more than a couple of minutes at most to get the bag but by then, when he came back with Tommo, whom he'd met in the courtyard, it was too late to save Irena. She was lying on the floor with her face blue and her tongue lolling out and her skirts ruckled up around her fat white thighs, a dead, ungainly lump of flesh on the dank flagstones. Even at that moment, he found her too repellent to excite in him any sort of compassion, or any kind of remorse for what he'd done.

What he did feel was fear at his own loss of control, and the need to get rid of her and, overriding everything else, a desire to flee. Blinking, he saw that they had all now reassembled in the hall—Tommo, as well as Madeleine and Angie, who was crouching in the corner and whimpering like a frightened kitten. And Sophie. Looking at him with an expression he couldn't bear to face.

It was the silence, after the tumult of the last few minutes, which unnerved him most. Nobody was saying anything, until a hoarse voice he didn't for the moment recognize as his own broke in, demanding help, asking what could be done to get rid of her.

It astonished him afterwards, thinking about it, that not one of them had jibbed at that. At the time, it had seemed quite natural for them to agree. None of them, after all, wanted to hurt Kitty and bring trouble to her door, which was what would happen if Irena Bron's death became public. In addition, and more urgently, they all had their own personal reasons for wanting it kept quiet: it would have done Madeleine's career, and the hospital campaign she'd begun to work for, no good at all to be involved in such a scandal, blameless though she was. And Sophie . . . Hope had momentarily risen in his breast: perhaps she was fond of him, after all, fond enough not to want him to be found out. As for Tommo—he had a past, something he wouldn't want revealed in the light of the publicity that would be certain to follow. There had been that woman reporter coming to the house looking for him, asking questions. She hadn't found him, for Kitty had sent her away with a flea in her ear, but Felix, keeping a jealous eye on him, had noted the hunted look on Tommo's face ever since.

Angie, Felix had disregarded, knowing she'd go along with anything Madeleine decided to do. And in that it seemed he'd made his most terrible mistake.

He thought that what had swayed them most of all was the knowledge that Irena was due to leave first thing in the morning, her bags packed, her farewells to Kitty already made. One of them, they decided, would write a letter to her new employers, as if from her. Nobody would ever miss her. And in the end, it hadn't taken long, all of them playing their part, to get rid of the thing that had been Irena Bron: to wrap her in plastic refuse bags, secure her with nylon rope, weight her down and dump her in the lake. Tommo had undertaken to get rid of her suitcases later.

After that, everyone had gone home and he, Felix, had thrown himself on his bed, still fully dressed, and slept until dawn, when he packed his things in his duffel bag, breakfasted and walked down the drive of Flowerdew without a backward glance to wait for the taxi which had been ordered to take Irena to the station.

'We put her down by the jetty of the old boathouse, wedged her between the stanchions. It would've been better to take her to the middle, where it's deeper, but we'd no way of getting her there. The old boat was no good, Tommo and I had been meaning to repair it but had never got around to it.'

So far, Mayo had had no difficulty in believing what Darbell had said: it tied in with what he'd already learned, with Angie Robinson's letter and with what the other people concerned had told him, or not told him, as the case might be. He found the explanation of how Irena Bron had come to die easy enough to believe, and even—to a certain extent —why they had all been at such pains to collude in concealing her death. But the next part—!

He read the second half of Darbell's statement through again with the same jaundiced disbelief he'd felt when he first listened to the man making it, well able to understand why Darbell had been reluctant to tell the story. On the other hand, it was so bizarre that Mayo felt no one in his right mind would have invented it as an excuse for being in Lavenstock, and gradually he began to have a strong feeling that somewhere within that unlikely story was concealed the nub of this case.

He picked up the typed pages and began to read again.

Darbell stated that having read the manuscript he had found in the envelope handed to him at the hotel, and seen the terse command at the end: *8.00 p.m. 13a, Bulstrode Street, Lavenstock, Tuesday 10th March. Be there*, he had immediately realized what was happening—that he was, in effect, being blackmailed:

'I could at first think of only one person who might have written the manuscript—Sophie Amhurst, who had had ambitions to be a writer. But no way could I believe she was attempting to blackmail me. It was not in Sophie's nature as I remembered her. I did not intend giving in to blackmail in any shape or form, but I was furiously angry and wanted to know who the writer was. I decided to go to Bulstrode Street to find out for myself. I arrived in Lavenstock about four-thirty, and drove out to Flowerdew. I can't say why I decided to do this, except that I had time to spare and felt a compulsion to see it again. I only stayed a few minutes, there was no point in staying longer as the place was obviously empty and deserted. I was still much too early for the eight p.m. rendezvous at Bulstrode Street, so on impulse I drove out to Pennybridge, to the Amhurst family home, on the offchance of finding where Sophie

Amhurst was now living. I discovered that although she had married since then, she still lived there when she was in England, and was in fact there at that very moment. We talked for nearly an hour. I left at seven forty-five, convinced that she had not written the manuscript.

'From there, I drove straight to Bulstrode Street and found the door of the flat ajar but nobody there. A note had been left inviting me to wait and to help myself to a drink, which I did, and that is how my prints came to be on the whisky bottle. I waited for half an hour and then I left, leaving a message with the woman in the downstairs flat. When I learned that it was Angie Robinson who lived upstairs, I was inclined to dismiss the whole things as a hoax. I remembered Angie as a rather stupid woman and I had no doubts about being able to deal with her threats.

'I freely admit to having killed Irena Bron, under extreme provocation, but I did not kill Angie Robinson. Immediately I left her flat, I drove home. I did not at any time see her or speak to her.'

In fact, Felix had had not one, but several, very large drinks from the whisky bottle while waiting to meet his unknown correspondent, feeling he needed them before facing whatever was to come. Unused to alcohol in such quantity nowadays, it had made him very drunk, and he'd had no clear idea of events after leaving the flat, or of how he'd arrived home. He didn't, however, see the necessity to make things worse for himself by admitting this to the police.

Coffee was sent for and Mayo prepared to go over the evidence with Cherry once more. Cherry sat at ease in Mayo's chair, a spruce, bandbox figure, looking more like a parliamentary private secretary than a policeman. Sometimes Mayo thought he was more politician than policeman these days. He was ambitious, and he'd no intention, in the interests of his career if nothing else, of allowing this

investigation into Angie Robinson's death to reach stale-
mate.

Mayo stood by the window, hands stuck in his pockets,
looking out at his least favourite view. They were erecting
scaffolding around the Town Hall. Maybe they were going
to clean it and improve his outlook. He abandoned the
prospect without much difficulty and, since his chair was
already occupied, went to perch on the corner of his desk,
and switched on his desk lamp.

'So he reckons he's been framed,' Cherry said, tapping
immaculately manicured fingers on the desk. 'I'd give a lot
to see that manuscript he claims was substituted.'

'The guy's a lunatic, he says he put it through his office
shredder. Didn't want it to get into the wrong hands,
though he swears it contained nothing more than he's
already told us—but then he would, wouldn't he? As soon
as I mentioned Flowerdew he caved in. He must've known
that sooner or later, when it came to being questioned, one
or other of that lot was going to spill the beans. They might
for one reason or another have ganged up to protect him
at the time but that sort of loyalty only goes so far. He's
admitting to the Bron murder because he knows he's less
to lose. He's claiming provocation and hoping to get done
only for manslaughter, whereas the Robinson one was obviously premeditated—and he's categorically denying any
involvement in that.'

'How far is he to be believed?'

'Hell, I don't know! He's a tricky customer, too damn
smooth by half—but come to that, I don't trust the rest
of 'em, either. Together or singly. Working alone or in
cahoots. And if,' Mayo added broodingly, 'Darbell's as
innocent of Robinson's murder as he claims, the question
of who *did* murder her still remains.'

'He's the only one with a credible motive. She was evidently putting the screws on him and he silenced her,'
Cherry said with conviction. 'Keep at him, he can't hold

out for ever.' He thought for a moment or two, then said, more cautiously, 'Is it feasible that Angie Robinson could have written that manuscript he claims someone wished on him?'

'She was clever enough, or so we're given to understand. Anyway, I don't think any great expertise was demanded. According to Darbell, the manuscript was simply a fictionalized account of what actually happened the night Irena Bron was murdered.'

Cherry blew out his lips, more disbelieving than ever. 'Why fictionalize it?'

'Maybe because Sophie Lawrence was known to have had ambitions to be a writer. Darbell had been in love with her. When he read it, presumably, she would come to mind as having written it and that would bring him to Lavenstock.'

'I'm having problems in believing this, Gil! Nobody would go through all that rigmarole just to fit Darbell up!'

Common sense told Mayo the same thing. 'Maybe not. Maybe not one person. But three of them together . . . ?' He broke off. They'd been through all this before and he was only slightly less sceptical than Cherry. 'If it did happen like that, we're back to motive, aren't we? What could have been so imperative *to all three of them* that they should need to kill Angie Robinson and agree to let Darbell take the blame?'

One by one he'd interviewed them and taken their statements. All three had categorically denied being concerned in any way in the killing of Angie Robinson of course, but he'd made sure they had a rough passage before being charged with their part in the disposal of Irena Bron's body, breathing fire and brimstone in a way he rarely did. But then, rarely had he been so infuriated at having his time wasted, being led up the garden path. They were like three children, playing games. Somebody had to tell them there was a real world out here. Their case had been adjourned;

they were on bail for the moment but would have to appear on further charges. None of them would escape the publicity they had tried so hard to avoid; even their attempts to conceal the truth from Kitty Wilbraham had been disastrous. She would have to know now.

'And yet,' he mused, 'if it was Darbell, I can't believe he'd be such a fool as to leave his dabs over everything and to let Mrs Kitchener know he was there—unless he was totally out of his mind at what he'd done. Why go to the flat at all? Apart from the fact we've found no evidence to suggest she was killed there, there'd be all that difficulty of getting her downstairs and into her car—which wasn't parked near. They've been over Darbell's Jag with a fine-tooth comb and there's no evidence of her ever being in it.'

Back once more to the hypothesis of some sort of conspiracy. If they'd conspired once, they could do it again. And yet . . . he could envisage all of them playing separate parts, and he could see Thomas killing someone in a blind rage, given the right amount of provocation . . . but taking part in a cold-blooded, premeditated arrangement to murder Angie Robinson? And what about the rape?

'A sexual crime for a non-sexual reason?' Abigail said. 'But she wasn't raped, sir, was she?'

'Strangled, though,' Atkins said, 'and Thomas did help to cover up Irena Bron's murder, so he had a motive.'

'Of sorts,' said Mayo absently, looking at Abigail and feeling a slight prickling sensation at the back of his neck.

They had chapter and verse on Thomas now. He had preferred to be known as Tommo, not simply because of his dislike of his feminine-sounding Christian name, but because his full name was Maryon Glenister Thomas. As soon as Abigail mentioned his real name, bells had rung for Mayo, though the man had been generally known as Glen Thomas. 'I was still working in the North then, and I wasn't personally concerned with the investigation but I remember the stir it caused. Just refresh my memory on the details, Abigail.'

'He was in his early twenties, married, but playing around with a woman who ran a rather up-market fashion business. His wife found out and went and shot the other woman. There was enormous publicity. She was convicted of manslaughter and he had to take a lot of stick—and why not? He wasn't exactly blameless.'

Why not, indeed? But as far as Mayo remembered it the wife herself hadn't been entirely without blame, either; she too had played the field. It was a sordid affair altogether. He could understand why Thomas had changed his name and buried himself in that cottage, yet scandals like that never died down, but tended to follow wherever you went. The reporter Darbell had met snooping around—it was about the time Thomas's wife had been released to much public outrage, after serving only three years of her sentence, on the grounds of good behaviour. Thomas wouldn't want all that raked up again—it would be disagreeable, but it hardly constituted a motive for murdering Angie Robinson.

'I want this wrapped up, Gil,' had been Cherry's parting shot. 'Darbell obviously killed Robinson and it shouldn't be beyond the wit of man to prove it.'

All very well, but if Darbell was charged with Angie Robinson's murder on the evidence so far, he might well get away with it. If charged with Irena Bron's murder, Mayo might well be left with another unsolved murder on his hands.

CHAPTER 17

'So you've come to see me at last?'

Only now could Mayo truly believe Kitty Wilbraham was alive, now that he could see the evidence of it with his own eyes. At the back of his mind had been the ridiculous feeling that somehow, she had to be dead.

It was almost as difficult to believe she was over ninety, though she was a strange, small, desiccated creature. She was dressed in a floor-length dark blue caftan sewn with tarnished metal threads, her head bound with a twisted silk scarf low on her forehead. Barbaric ornaments depended from her ears—very similar to the earrings she had given Angie Robinson—and hung around her neck and her thin, chicken-bone wrists. Her hands in contrast were swollen and knotted with arthritis, and her skin hung in loose folds around her neck as if she had once been very fat. But her eyes were as alive and as alert as someone twenty years her junior. He wondered, looking at the embroidered slippers emerging from under her robe, if she had dolled herself up in this bizarre manner solely for their benefit or if it was her normal mode of dress. Abigail, whom he had brought with him in case Mrs Wilbraham became upset under his questioning, looking sensible and ordinary in her nice green suit, clear-eyed and intelligent, was a great relief.

'Do have some tea. Jessie has left some in the Thermos jug there, it's Earl Grey. I take it you'd prefer that to mint tea?'

Abigail said quickly, with an inquiring lift of the eyebrow towards Mayo, 'Earl Grey, thank you. It would be very nice.'

Mrs Wilbraham had chosen to see them here in the red room, the contents of which had so horrified Angie Robinson, although on this bright afternoon, with the sun throwing dusty greenish reflections from the lake outside, the room's richness appeared merely tawdry. But in the evening, when the pierced ceramic lamps were lit, and the reflections of the grinning masks, the urns and ceramic panels and the carved, obelisk-shaped objects threw grotesque shadows on to the lurid red walls, Mayo could envisage a most sinister ambience, capable of invoking the echoes of past horrors to someone as susceptible as Angie had been. Even he had to remind himself that they were only replicas; that their significance was all in the mind.

The old lady waited until they had availed themselves of tea before saying, 'Jessie Crowther tells me that tiresome gel Angie Robinson has got herself murdered. I assume that's why you're here—but what can it have to do with me?'

'When someone dies in suspicious circumstances, we have to go back a long way, Mrs Wilbraham, and she did occasionally visit here, we've been told.'

'Very occasionally. She was of limited appeal to me—I did not encourage her.'

'I'd like to talk about another matter first,' he said, uncomfortably conscious of the dry heat of the airless room, stuffy with Kairouan carpets on the mosaic-tiled floor and couches and ottomans heaped with cushions. Sweat was beginning to prickle out over his body. 'What can you tell me about Irena Bron?'

If the name had startled the old woman, she gave no sign. She stared at him impassively from the depths of her high-seated armchair that was designed for easy rising, but was also a little like a throne in this room, an illusion made more apparent by the carved, mother-of-pearl and ivory-studded screen behind it and the huge mask of the goddess Tanit on the wall above. She was like an ancient lizard, unmoving, unblinking, except for the eyes, black and alive and missing nothing. Not much like the warm-hearted, amusing, gregarious woman she'd been described as.

'Irena?' A sigh escaped her. 'That's a name I haven't heard for a long time.'

'Exactly how long, Mrs Wilbraham?'

'Exactly? That's a tall order for someone of my age, young man! My memory isn't what it was.'

This was evidently a pronouncement not meant to be taken seriously. Everything about her said she was still sharp as a needle. Moreover, there were indications that she was still working: writing materials were spread out over a table in the corner, there was even a small tape-recorder, presumably because she would find writing or typing difficult with those arthritic fingers. He suspected she had lost none of her critical faculties and that her memory was as clear as ever.

'I haven't set eyes on Irena for something like fourteen or fifteen years. Has she done something she shouldn't?'

'That would surprise you?'

'Nothing about Irena would surprise me,' she answered drily. 'She was a law entirely unto herself. No steadfastness of purpose, she'd just as soon act on a whim of the moment . . . But you must be fair with me and tell me what this is all about, otherwise, I warn you, you won't get a word out of me.'

He saw that he must tell her the truth immediately. She would have to know soon, anyway. He supposed that a person who had reached the age of fourscore years and ten must have learned to live with and accept the idea of bereavement and death, their own and that of those close to them—but she might have loved Irena Bron and be devastated, how could he know?

He told her as gently as he could that Irena Bron, too, was dead, and that he had come to seek permission to look for her body in the lake. It did not seem to upset her as much as he had feared it might, though she closed her eyes momentarily as though against a spasm of pain.

'Dead?' she murmured, almost to herself. 'I knew it had to be so.'

'You knew, Mrs Wilbraham?'

'Tell me,' she countered. 'Tell me everything.'

'I would prefer to ask a few questions first.'

She shrugged and spread her misshapen hands. He saw that they trembled very slightly, with age or apprehension, it wasn't possible to tell. 'Very well.'

'Who was she?' Mayo began. 'And how did she come to be living here?'

'She was the daughter of Miloslav Bron, a man my husband and I worked with for several years in Tunisia, before the war. We lost touch during the war. And then one day Irena appeared on my doorstep with a suitcase, saying her father was dead and had left her penniless. That was no surprise. Milo's nature was always feckless.'

She delivered the judgement reprovingly, but a barely perceptible smile lifted the corners of her mouth and there was a long pause, as if she had travelled far away in her mind. Mayo had to bring her back to the present with a gentle prod: 'She stayed with you?'

'Irena? Oh yes. He had left a letter, you see, recommending her to me, rather like a helpless child—though she was nearly forty and more than capable of fending for herself! However, for his sake, I willingly gave her a temporary home. Look behind you, on the chest. You'll see a photo that might interest you. If you've seen Milo, you've seen Irena.'

Abigail picked up the framed snapshot, glanced at it and passed it over to Mayo. 'That's my husband, the bearded one,' the old woman said with pride. 'He was Dr Alfred Wilbraham. I don't suppose you've heard of him unless you're particularly interested in archæology, but he was in his day one of the most eminent people in his field.'

The photo must have been taken fifty or more years ago, at some archæological dig in the desert. The camera had caught Kitty and Miloslav Bron laughing together, with the short and stocky, plus-foured Alfred Wilbraham standing a little apart. Bron looked dashing and swarthily handsome; the young Kitty, with an abundance of curling hair and an impish smile, was pretty and petite. The two looked as though they were used to sharing laughter.

'How long did Irena Bron stay here?'

'In the event, eighteen months. I never had any intention

of supporting her indefinitely and she was, I must admit, difficult to live with at times. I was quite relieved when she announced she had obtained a position in the City and was leaving.'

'What do you think made her decide to leave?'

'I have no idea. Madeleine Freeman suggested it and I suppose it just appealed to her at the time. She was a creature of whim.'

'She left on August the fifteenth, 1979, to be precise? And you gave a farewell dinner for her the night previously?'

She raised to her lips the glass of mint tea that stood by her side and sipped. 'If you say so. I don't really remember, it's all so long ago. It would have been somewhere around that date, I imagine.'

'And the others who were present were,' Mayo said, ticking them off on his fingers, 'Madeleine Freeman and Angie Robinson, your handyman, Thomas? Yes? Felix Darbell?' She nodded. 'And Sophie Amhurst?'

'Yes, Sophie, too.' At the roll-call of names she smiled and he saw the charisma was still there after all. It was easier now to see why they had loved her, all those young people she had drawn around her, and why they had wanted to protect her, keeping Irena's death from her.

'I'm going to have to ask you to tell me what happened that night, Mrs Wilbraham.'

'Nothing happened, that I recall. I was very tired and went to bed early.'

'We've been told there was some trouble, some sort of table-tapping session, ending in a quarrel.'

'I know nothing about that, I was in bed,' she repeated stubbornly.

He had no option but to accept what she said. 'Did you hear from Irena after she left your house?' She shook her head. 'Not even a letter?'

'No.'

'And you didn't think of making inquiries?'

She made a gesture of impatience. 'She might have been anywhere in the world, any of the places she'd lived in before she came to me. She—and her father—were like gipsies, never staying in any place for long. No, I was too old, even then, to go to all the bother of making inquiries.'

'Forgive me, but I noticed it didn't surprise you to learn she was dead?'

'When you've lived as long as I have, very little surprises you.' She began to speak quickly so that her words slurred slightly. 'It's difficult to remember after all this time but yes, I think I began to believe she must be. I realized even Irena would not be silent for so long. Irena less than anyone, perhaps. I never knew a woman more voluble, in at least three languages! I'm afraid I used to find her tiresome on the whole, an excitable sort of temperament, you know, though that was only to be expected, considering her background . . .' She broke off with a sigh. She was beginning to look very tired, and alarmingly flushed across her cheekbones. 'More tea, Mr Mayo, Miss Moon? Please help yourselves.'

How much of what she's said was true, or how much had she come to believe it was? She hadn't asked for details of how Irena Bron had died and he wondered if she had quite understood what his request about the lake meant. When Abigail had performed the rites with their teacups, he said, 'You do understand that Irena's death was not due to natural causes?'

'If you're going to drag the lake, I assume it wasn't,' she answered, suddenly sharp. 'But Irena, I assure you, was *not* the sort to take her own life. It must have been an accident.'

There was a pause. Mayo said, 'Felix Darbell has confessed to her murder.'

It was a long time before she spoke. 'Has he indeed?' she said at last. 'Well, he never liked her. He thought she was after my money when I died.' She added with a brief, wintry smile, 'They all did.'

Money. Never far behind, money. And because the house was neglected and decaying and the two old women lived a frugal existence, it didn't mean there wasn't any. Did Kitty's wealth lurk there, in the background, as the key to all this? Another idea occurred to him. Was it possible that Irena Bron had been Kitty's daughter, the result of a liaison with the dashing Miloslav Bron? Was that why she had put up with her for so long?

'And was she, ma'am?' he asked bluntly. 'After your money?'

'I'd have soon sent her packing, if she had been!'

And so vehemently was it said that he immediately dismissed the idea of a mother/daughter connection. Yet this question had disturbed her. She was avoiding looking at him and her gaze was travelling slowly round the room, resting briefly on her treasures as if they were, ultimately, the only things left to draw comfort from. 'Murder,' she repeated, 'that's a very terrible thing.'

He said bluntly, 'What made you leave Flowerdew so suddenly, ma'am, and return to Tunisia? Immediately after Irena had gone?'

'Oh,' she returned, shrugging, 'why does one do anything? I wanted to go, so why not? That's the consolation of age, one is no longer bound by convention. It doesn't matter now, anyway. And now, I'm sorry, I'm very tired, you'll have to excuse me. I'm really too old for all this. Recalling the past can be very exhausting.'

Mayo stood up immediately and so did Abigail. It was difficult to discern whether she really was too tired to go on, or was simply making excuses to get rid of them, but she had been for the most part cooperative and he had to accept her dismissal. He wasn't in the business of intimidating old ladies. Besides, when you'd lived nigh on a hundred years, he reckoned you were entitled to tell nosey-parker coppers to shove off when you'd had enough of them. He would come again with more questions and hope to find out just what it was she was concealing.

'Thank you for seeing us, Mrs Wilbraham. I'm sorry we've had to trouble you.'

When they were at the door, her voice spoke behind them. 'But you haven't told me what all this has to do with Angie Robinson? Has—has Felix murdered her, too?'

He considered her for a moment. 'He swears that he didn't.'

She contemplated her swollen hands, crossed in her lap. 'Poor Felix. He was always his own worst enemy.' There was a frozen look on her old face as she raised it. 'I suppose it's always easier the second time.'

Soon after that, a flurry of activity began by the old boat-house; frogmen arrived with their gear, the pathologist came, and a clutch of detectives. Police vehicles and the ambulance blocked the road outside the house. Finally, the lake at Flowerdew surrendered its secrets. What was left of Irena Bron was recovered from its murky depths. The old house, which had probably seen much worse in its long history, slumbered on.

CHAPTER 18

By this time Angie Robinson's bank manager had at last returned from whatever business (or pleasure) had been keeping him away, and Mayo managed to fix up an interview with him. He was called Smythe, a youngish man of rather stout proportions, who took himself seriously and sported mutton-chop whiskers like Abraham Lincoln or Mr Murdstone. A harmless affectation, the whiskers gave him a certain weighty authority by putting years on his age and boosting his trustworthiness rating by several points.

'We—the bank, that is—are her executors,' Smythe told him, intimating that he would be willing to cooperate in the matter of letting Angie's affairs be known. 'How can I help you?'

The first thing Mayo learned was that Angie Robinson had deposited all her personal papers with the bank several weeks ago, which explained their absence among her personal effects. The second was that there was a very substantial amount of money in her account, and that she'd either been financially astute or had been well-advised in the management of it. In addition to a sizeable capital on which interest had accrued, there were stocks, shares and investment trusts bringing in further dividends. Her salary from the Area Health Authority had been paid in monthly, and her outgoings were modest, apart from a large withdrawal recently to finance the purchase of her new Astra. If her intention had been to blackmail Felix Darbell, it appeared to have been for reasons other than a need for money, though where the capital had come from in the first place was a question to which Mayo would need an answer.

'There's also the property, of course,' added Smythe, presenting him with the answer before he asked.

'Property? Which property?'

'The house where she lived in Kilbracken Road, for a start. That should fetch a reasonable price when the market looks up again. There's a continuing demand for that sort of substantial family house. Not too big, though I dare say it'll need a bit of modernizing—new bathrooms and so on. I don't think Miss Robinson's ever done anything of that sort. Just as her parents left it.'

Mayo had been in the game long enough not to be surprised for long at anything he heard but there was always something that could knock you off your peg. After a moment, he said, 'I was under the impression it belonged to Dr Freeman.'

'I don't know who gave you that information. It came to Angela Robinson nearly twenty years ago, after her parents died. In fact, Joseph Robinson's father left it to *him*, as well as the business.'

'What business was that?' Mayo asked carefully.

It turned out to be Robinson's Hardware in the High Street, a shop Mayo passed every day of his life. 'You must know it,' Smythe said, 'they're still trading under that name, though none of the family are now concerned. Joseph Robinson sold it shortly before he died . . . which meant there was still a tidy sum left for his daughter. As for the house,' he added, stroking his luxuriant whiskers in the approved Victorian manner, 'Dr Freeman will be able to stay there until such time as she decides to leave . . . I understand she's getting married shortly. The contents will, of course, now have to be sold as well.'

'Who's the beneficiary? Dr Freeman?'

'No. Everything goes to a charity—to the Leukæmia Fund, as it happens.'

Not a bean to the Women's Hospital. And before Mayo left, Smythe lobbed another grenade into his lap. 'The house in Bulstrode Street, by the way. That will be sold, too, of course, but as a business proposition, which was why Joseph Robinson bought it. Sadly, now,' he added, 'with vacant possession of the top-floor flat.'

Mayo was willing to concede that it was not Madeleine Freeman's fault that he had assumed the Kilbracken Road house to be hers—although she'd said nothing to contradict his assumption. He could only conclude it was probably a harmless bit of snobbery to let him think she owned it, particularly if, say, she'd come from a less affluent background than Angie.

But why had Angie, with all her resources, chosen to leave her home and live in Bulstrode Street, of all places?

'Pique,' said Abigail Moon.

'Pique?'

'Jealousy because Madeleine Freeman was getting married. After all, they'd spent most of their lives in each other's pockets—she was Angie's only friend as far as we know—and Angie seems to have been the sort of person who wouldn't hesitate to make anyone feel bad for leaving her in the lurch. You know the sort of thing: *"How am I going to manage, all on my little own? I can't stay here rattling around in this place all by myself, it's not fair. Look what you've reduced me to."* Even though it was supposed to be only temporary until she bought herself something nicer. She could've got a lot of mileage out of that, playing the martyr.'

It was a shrewd guess that filled in with what they'd learned of Angie Robinson's character. And it was the only explanation Mayo could think of for anyone going to live in Bulstrode Street who didn't absolutely have to.

'George,' he said, 'did you know Angie Robinson was one of the same family as Robinson's Hardware?'

'Robinson's Hardware?' echoed George Atkins. 'No, I didn't.' His knowledge of Lavenstock, its villains, its customs, and all the people who lived therein was legendary and he was mortified that he hadn't previously made the connection between the murdered woman and the shop, although there was no reason why he should have done so. 'I know it was started by old Spencer Robinson and carried on by his son Joe. And he's been dead donkey's years.'

'Was he the sort to knock his wife and child about?'

'Joe Robinson? Nah! Never! The last man—!' Atkins stopped, running his hand over his grizzled head, his expression rueful. 'Wish I'd a pound for every man I've said that about and been proved wrong! Who knows what goes on between four walls? But Joe Robinson? Can't say it's impossible, mind—but I'd be surprised.'

'What do you know about Dr Freeman's background? She and Angie went to the same school, so she must be local.'

Atkins shook his head. 'Not from the town, I reckon. Maybe one of the villages. I can find out.'

'Do, when you've time. As a matter of interest.'

Mayo began to be haunted by a sense of failure and a feeling that there was something, somewhere, that he had noticed subconsciously and not remembered, something just outside his grasp, like a shadow on the mind.

The trouble was, they had incidentally solved one murder they hadn't known had been committed, but he was still left with the original unsolved murder on his hands.

He could not accept that the two were unconnected. Somewhere there was a pattern that linked them, a chain of events that had been set in motion by Irena Bron's death. This murder of Angie Robinson was where it had all started for him and he was damned if it was going to go down as one of the unsolved crimes of the twentieth century.

He shrugged on his jacket and left word that he was going home.

Outside it was a cold, hard night and the sky was thick with stars. Already the pavements were sparkling with frost. He took deep breaths of the sharp, invigorating air, welcome as wine after the grossly overheated premises he'd just left and felt the need all at once to stretch his legs before the drive home.

Mayo's habit of striding around the town at all times of the day or night, sometimes even in the small hours, was something he was well known for by now. He wasn't always welcomed, not only by the criminal fraternity but sometimes by members of the strength who were skiving a crafty half-hour off duty, or pursuing leisure activities they'd rather he didn't know about. But that didn't stop Mayo. He saw the town in all its moods, knew its dark corners and its short cuts, what went on in its pubs and clubs and the twice-weekly market. He was sometimes able to anticipate where trouble was likely to occur.

Tonight his walk was more purposeful than usual, taking him up Hill Street and past the old chapel—*Ebenezer Methodist Chapel. All welcome*, it still said on the board outside. He paused outside the little forecourt to read it, listening to the roar of the ring road in the distance as it skirted Bulstrode Street. He walked the hundred yards or so up to the car park at the Women's Hospital and two or three minutes later passed the end of Kilbracken Road, where the house with its *For Sale* notice stood dark, its curtains undrawn across its blank windows. By the time he emerged into the High Street again, thoughts were beginning to stir; the pattern he had been seeking was beginning to form in his mind, but it was not one that made him feel any better.

Turning towards Milford Road and the station car park, food smells assailed him on all sides, steamy wafts from the chippie and assorted savoury odours from the Lotus Blossom, the Burger King and the pizza palace on the corner, and he was suddenly seized by hunger, realizing that he hadn't had a square meal for days and nothing at all since his sketchy breakfast. He pushed open the door of the Saracen's, deciding to stop off there for supper.

The first people he saw inside were DC Spalding and someone it took him a moment or two to register as Abigail Moon, her hair loose and falling in a coppery curtain to her shoulders. Even in the brief glimpse he had of the couple he felt the intensity of their absorption. It was a situation he had never envisaged and didn't want to know about. The last thing he needed at the moment was personal involvement among his team, of the sort likely to bring disruption to the investigation. He didn't think they'd seen him and went to sit with his back to them in one of the curtained booths facing the door. It wasn't a seat he would have otherwise chosen. It was in a draught and he was on full view from the foyer. He ordered a half of bitter and a grilled steak, little knowing he'd been witness to the last throes of their affair.

*

'Don't look now,' Abigail said, 'but the Gaffer's just come in. I don't think he's seen us. We can go out the other way.'

'Stay where you are,' Spalding said intensely, by now in no mood for retreat. 'We've a perfect right to be here. And we're still in the middle of a discussion, remember?'

'We've said everything there is to say,' she said wearily. They'd been bickering like this for half an hour. It was a situation that would have been ludicrous had it not been so painful—both feeling guilty for not feeling guilty enough.

She drained the last of her orange juice. 'I saw Roz at Pennybridge this afternoon.'

It took a lot to make him lose his temper, but Abigail had succeeded. 'You did *what*? You deliberately went and discussed me with my wife?'

'No, not deliberately. I had to check Sophie's alibi with her—and she was the one who broached the subject. I don't know how she knew who I was—she just cottoned on, I suppose. Nick,' she said, suddenly urgent, 'there's still a chance for you two to get your act together, as long as you'll try and compromise a bit.'

'Compromise? That's rich, coming from you! When did you ever compromise with anything, especially your bloody career—and that's what it all boils down to, isn't it?'

This was where they'd come in. She knew from experience he could go on indefinitely in this way and suddenly she'd had enough. 'Listen,' she said, and proceeded to tell him in words of only syllable exactly what she felt. It was hurtful, it wasn't kind, but he let her go on and didn't try to stop her when she left.

It had, after all, given him the escape route he wanted.

A function was being held in the large dining-room at the back of the hotel and groups of well-heeled people in evening dress were milling around in the foyer. In one such group was a solicitor by the name of Crytch with whom

Mayo was acquainted. He raised his hand to Mayo across the foyer and spoke to one of his companions. While the women in their party were being directed to the cloakroom, the man who'd been spoken to excused himself and came across to where Mayo sat. A stranger to him, he was a distinguished-looking man with a direct and decisive look, wearing with his superbly-cut dinner suit a dark velvet cummerbund and bow tie that enhanced a pair of startlingly vivid blue eyes.

'Chief Inspector Mayo?' Mayo nodded, half rose. 'My name's Bouvier, Edward Bouvier. May I have a few words with you? I shan't keep you long, we're due to dine in fifteen minutes.'

'Please do. How can I help you, Mr Bouvier?' Mayo said, grasping the proffered hand and waving to the opposite seat.

'Thank you. We haven't met before but you may have heard of me . . . Dr Freeman is my fiancée.'

'I remember the name.'

Despite his direct initial approach it took the man a moment or two to get round to what he had to say. 'I—er —just wanted a few words with you about this wretched business.' He had a deep and pleasant voice, with a very slight accent that Mayo was unable to place. He looked authoritative and sure of himself, which was not how he sounded. 'I guess you won't be aware of this, but I'm going back to Montreal to take up a consultancy there in a few weeks.'

'Canada? You're not getting married, then?'

It had been the first thing Mayo had thought, and perhaps it wasn't appropriate. The other man stared. 'Oh, sure, Madeleine's going, too. We've already put out feelers for an appointment for her there. That surprises you?'

'I'm surprised to hear that she's prepared to leave the Women's Hospital—and everything she's worked for.'

'If I know Madeleine, she'll find some other cause to

replace it,' Bouvier said drily. 'But it's like this—so far, that's been the most important thing in her life and if she wins she'll have achieved her aim—so what's left? On the other hand, if she loses, and frankly . . .' He hesitated. 'Frankly, I never could see her having a cat in hell's chance of winning this damn crusade and that's why I want her away. She'd take it very badly indeed if she had to stay here and live with failure, so Canada seems the answer.'

'Mr Bouvier, she's on bail pending trial. It'll be up to the court to decide what happens about that.'

He looked suddenly grey. 'She's a fine woman. In view of her record of devoted service—'

'I shouldn't bank on it.'

He burst out suddenly, 'I'll never believe she did what she did for other than the best of motives. If it hadn't been for Angie Robinson's murder, that business all those years ago would never have come to light, and several people's lives might not have been wrecked. Everything's down to that woman. I naturally deplore what's happened to her, but I can't help being glad her influence on Madeleine has stopped.'

It was an interesting view of morality, and it contained what was news to Mayo, that Madeleine Freeman had been in any way influenced by Angie Robinson. Everything so far had pointed to it being the other way round. He sipped his beer and waited for the other man to expound, always willing to be enlightened.

'Perhaps influence is the wrong word. But they had a very—complicated relationship, she's never been able to see quite straight about Angie. She's normally very sensible and clear-sighted but she seems to have had a blind spot about that woman—just as she does about the hospital. But every time I tried to make Madeleine see she'd better believe that, there was Angie Robinson, egging her on, encouraging her, knowing all the time that it was bound to be a miserable failure.'

'Carry on, Mr Bouvier, you interest me. Why do you think she did that?'

Bouvier consulted his watch. 'I must go,' he said, but making no move to do so, in fact leaning further back into the plush banquette seat. He fingered his bow tie with the smallish, yet strong and precise hands of the true surgeon, repeating quietly, 'Why did she want Madeleine to fail? Because she was always jealous of her. It wasn't apparent, she was careful not to let it show, but perhaps I've been in a more privileged position than most people to be able to recognize it. She was, you know, really a very possessive, not to say destructive woman . . .'

The door into the foyer revolved as yet another laughing, chattering party entered. Bouvier waited until they had dispersed, then looked again at his watch, rose and held out his hand. 'My friends will be thinking me unpardonably rude. Thank you for listening to me—I felt I had to try and show you just what sort of woman Angie was.'

'Thank you, Mr Bouvier, I appreciate the effort.'

When he had gone, Mayo sat, sipping his beer, thinking about what had been said. His steak came. He ate it without relish. Somehow, he seemed to have lost his appetite.

Yet it was surprisingly easy after that, when he was at home, his feet up on the coffee table, a Scotch at his elbow, the Monteverdi *Vespers* on the turntable and the Irena Bron file resting on his knees, to see what had eluded him before.

Sophie Lawrence, Madeleine Freeman, Thomas. He read each of their statements in turn, all three of which had corroborated Felix Darbell's account of what had happened. None of them, he noted, had actually been there when Darbell had killed Irena. Madeleine had arrived too late to prevent it happening, Thomas had met Felix in the courtyard after the event, when he had gone to fetch Dr Freeman's bag, and Sophie had apparently come into the hall last of all. Their statements dovetailed and, combining with Darbell's, gave a clear picture of what had happened.

Once more he read through Sophie Lawrence's statement. He thought of the dank, shadowed hall at Flowerdew and the staircase rising into thickening darkness. He drank some whisky and listened to the luminous brilliance of the *Magnificat* soaring through the room. He waited until it had finished and then put through a call to Doc Ison.

Scarcely had he put the phone down after having had his theory confirmed before it rang again. It was Atkins. 'I've just had a call from an oppo of mine regarding that matter we spoke about . . .'

CHAPTER 19

The forensic report on the scrap of plastic caught in the earring was delivered by hand. Abigail took it straight up to Mayo's office and found him sitting with the suspect file open on his desk, his tie pulled loose, his jacket off, two cups half full of cold coffee by his elbow. Her entry seemed to galvanize him into action. Straightening his tie, he stood up and reached for his jacket, asking what was in the report.

'They think the scrap of plastic's probably come from one of those pac-a-mac things. Certainly not a dustbin liner as we thought.'

'And no doubt whoever it belongs to will have put it tidily away in their wardrobe, waiting for us to find it? Likely!'

'It wouldn't have been a remarkable thing for anyone to have worn it on a night like that. If it had a hood on it could've covered the killer from head to toe. That's why he left no traces in the Astra.'

'Yes.'

It was another dismal day, with a sky like pewter and the fluorescent lights on all over the building. Mayo thought for a moment. 'Get your coat, Abigail. It's time we stopped running about like headless chickens. Give me a minute or two and then I'll be with you. I just want a few words with George before we go.'

It was only eleven in the morning, yet Sophie Lawrence already had a drink in her hand (a tumbler filled with ice-cubes, topped with whisky, an American abomination to some, but that was how she liked it) when the bell rang. The sudden peal startled her and made her tremble, though it was almost certainly only Roz, who was making sure she wasn't left alone any longer than necessary these days. She was frightened of her own shadow lately and could see no reason why this state of affairs shouldn't continue to the end of her days, whatever was going to happen to her in the future. When she opened the door and saw who it was standing there, and saw their unsmiling faces, she knew she had reason to be afraid.

'May we come in, Mrs Lawrence?'

'You've caught me at a bad time, I'm afraid, Chief Inspector,' she said, taking a grip on herself, determined not to be intimidated. 'I was just going out—but come in for a moment.'

The golden room, lit by lamplight against the darkness of the morning, looked more luxurious than ever, like a TV setting for a period film, the woman in it almost as unreal, gold at her ears and wrists, soft, gleaming leather boots, her full, wine-coloured wool skirts a pool of colour around her feet as she sank on to a low chair by the fire.

'No drink for you, I presume—but I do have tea or coffee,' she offered, and when the offer was refused, she picked up her own drink rather defiantly and glanced at her wristwatch.

Mayo was in no mood to make apologies for keeping her. 'One or two questions, Mrs Lawrence,' was all he said.

'I thought we'd finished with all that. Isn't it time I was

left alone? I've admitted what happened—what more do you want?'

She had lost that slightly abstracted air and seemed in an indefinable way older and sadder, her features more finely drawn. But change of some kind was an inevitable legacy of murder, which never could be less than a violent intrusion, overturning the lives of those concerned, stamping them unalterably with its dark consequences so that they were never the same again.

'I think you'll find we've hardly begun—not on the subject of Angie Robinson's murder, at any rate,' he answered.

An anonymous, plodding sort of man, she'd thought the Chief Inspector—until that last, ghastly interview, when he'd met all her previous lies and evasions with a hard, uncompromising directness which made her acutely aware that he wasn't a man to be fooled around with.

But it was Abigail who began the questioning. 'Mrs Lawrence, we'd like to go over the statement you made—'

Before she could finish, the other woman interrupted. 'I ought to tell you. I—I made a mistake. I was talking to my sister and I suddenly remembered that I did go out that night—though it was after Felix had gone.'

A simultaneous realization occurred to Abigail and Mayo, that Sophie Lawrence had thought she was to be questioned again about Angie Robinson's murder and not, as they had intended, about Irena Bron's. Abigail adjusted her sights while Mayo said, his eyes flinty grey, 'It's taken you ten days to remember?'

'I didn't think it was that important—I'm sure it isn't —but Roz said it might be,' she answered. Apprehensively, it seemed to Abigail, however nonchalant she tried to appear.

'I think we'd better start at the beginning again. From the point where you went to see your sister earlier in the evening.' Mayo signified to Abigail that she should continue.

'It's not five minutes' walk across the green to your sister's house, Mrs Lawrence—but you drove there?' she began.

'Of course. It was pouring with rain.'

'Did you wear a mac?' Sophie blinked, then nodded. 'A plastic one?'

'*Plastic?*' Lady Bracknell could not have said it with more disdain. 'No. A Burberry. And I used an umbrella too, when I got out of the car. What *is* this?'

'You returned home, had a light supper, then just before seven o'clock, Mr Darbell arrived. You had coffee together and he left at seven forty-five. Have we got that correct?'

'That's what I've already said.' The ice clattered against the side of the glass as Sophie lifted it to her lips. 'And he's confirmed it.'

Did she really think she could cite Darbell as a reliable witness, Abigail wondered, but thought it prudent not to voice her opinion. 'So it was after that you went out again? Even though you'd previously said that you spent the rest of the evening here, alone?'

'Well, I don't suppose it's going to make any difference now, but yes, I did go out, though only for half an hour.' Her eyes were clear as dark amber, wide and honest. So Mayo had seen a hundred criminals, guilty as hell, look.

'Did you go down to Hill Street chapel?' he asked abruptly.

'Where?' She seemed genuinely bewildered. 'No. No, I —I drove down to see Madeleine Freeman but she wasn't in, so I came straight home again.'

'Suppose,' he said, at his most stolid, 'you tell us why you went to see Dr Freeman.'

She hesitated. 'After Felix had been to see me I needed to talk to her, to ask her advice. It was a shock, as you might imagine, when Felix turned up on my doorstep but although he stayed the best part of an hour he refused to tell me why he'd come back. It seemed to me he was in a very strange, dangerous sort of mood. He spoke about what had happened at Flowerdew, though only in an oblique sort of way, and when he'd gone, I began to think it might be that for some reason he'd taken it into his head to confess, and what that might mean for us.'

'What made you think that?'

'Madeleine had always been afraid that one day that might happen, that the need to confess might become overwhelming, you know.' She licked her lips and tried an appealing look from one to the other but encountered nothing to help her. 'Well, I thought she ought to know he'd come back, and she always knows what to do. As it happens, she wasn't in, so I rang her next day and we agreed to meet and talk it over.'

'By we, you mean yourself, Dr Freeman and Mr Thomas? And you met in the back premises of Oundle's Bookshop?' She looked startled, but nodded. 'And what was the result of this meeting?'

'Nothing. Because by then Angie had been murdered. There was nothing we could do except lie low and say nothing and hope you'd never trace Felix.'

For a long time Mayo didn't speak, then he put his hand in his pocket and stretched out his hand, palm uppermost, with the earring on it, and showed it to her, just as he had with Madeleine Freeman. 'Have you seen this before?'

Her hand went to her mouth. 'It was Irena's.'

'Irena Bron's? Are you certain?'

'Absolutely. They were a farewell present to her that last night. She put them straight on.'

'You're sure of that? Sure this is one of the same pair— and not just similar to the ones Mrs Wilbraham gave to Angie Robinson?'

'Angie Robinson? Kitty would never have given jewellery to Angie!' Sophie said. 'She wasn't exactly her favourite person. No, these were definitely Irena's.'

'You say Irena put them straight on, yet when we found

Irena's body, she wasn't wearing any jewellery.' She closed her eyes briefly. 'How do you account for that?'

'I can't. I had nothing to do with . . . with all that.' And a little desperately, 'And I'm sorry, but I really can't help you any more.'

'I think you can. I want you to repeat exactly what you remember about the circumstances of the murder, everything that happened after the quarrel broke out between Irena Bron and Felix Darbell.'

Unwillingly, at last, she said, 'Well, as I told you, after a few minutes Felix stormed out and Irena followed him. We could hear them in the hall, shouting, and then . . . then there was a crash and everything went quiet. A few seconds later, Madeleine ran out, and then Angie. I knew something terrible must have happened but I didn't seem to be able to move . . . When I did go into the hall, Irena was lying on the floor and Madeleine was standing beside her. Angie was crying. Then Felix came back with Tommo, bringing Madeleine's bag. She said, "I'm sorry, Felix, there was nothing I could do. I'm afraid she's dead."'

'And that's all? Are you sure you haven't forgotten anything? Anything at all that happened in the hall, no matter how trivial? *Think!* Go over the whole scene in your mind. Something you saw, maybe?' She shook her head vehemently. 'Or heard?

'Just a minute—yes! Yes, I remember now. It was before Felix went out, before Irena—'

'Yes?'

'We heard the boards creaking in the room above, Kitty moving about. We thought we'd disturbed her with all the noise. And then . . . just before . . . I heard her footsteps again. And the door banged . . .' Her voice trailed off. 'And that really is all I can remember.'

'Thank you, Mrs Lawrence.'

It wasn't exactly what he'd been hoping for, but it

confirmed what he'd been thinking, and it might prove to be enough.

It was scarcely more than an hour later when Sophie Lawrence, having thought long and hard, and having tipped what was still left of her whisky (most of it) wastefully, but wisely, down the sink, drove across Hartopp Moor and dropped down towards Flowerdew.

Leaving her car parked outside the gates, she walked up the drive, dismayed to find how neglected the house had become, and that it still exerted the same old magic. An evil magic, she had afterwards come to think it, and looking at the dark banefulness of the lake on this cold grey morning, remembering, she had to force herself not to believe that now.

CHAPTER 20

She knew her way, remembering every nook and cranny, every ingress and egress of Flowerdew, and was not going to be deflected from her purpose by being turned back ignominiously at the door. Things might have changed, but not so much that Jessie Crowther would deliberately disobey Kitty by not keeping her out—for such had been her orders. Sophie and Madeleine might never have learned of Kitty's return to Flowerdew, had it not been for recent events, although Tommo—and how this hurt!—had known all along. He had tried to make light of this by saying that Kitty wouldn't have told him, either, had she and Jessie not been dependent upon him for their very survival. But now, Sophie intended to see Kitty, come what may.

There were two places where the old women were likely to be. One was the kitchen, and the other the red room.

Tommo had said they kept the doors bolted and barred, but there was one way in to which she still had a key.

She knew the danger of letting herself in without being announced. She might antagonize Kitty further; the shock of seeing her might give the old woman a heart attack . . .

She moved quietly along the flagged path between the lake and the house . . .

Kitty was seated at her desk in the red room, dressed in one of her old blue kaftans. She was half-turned from the french window, reading, her spectacles half way down her nose and, for a moment, Sophie thought: She hasn't changed. She's exactly the same. And then something, a current of air perhaps, must have made her aware of the open window and she turned, one hand flew to her breast and she gave a small choking gasp. In the moment before Kitty recognized her, Sophie saw how the years had laid their burden on her, how the skin bore a fine network of wrinkles, like antique porcelain, how swollen and dreadfully knotted and misshapen her hands had become, and that her former stoutness had now given way to shapelessness only partly hidden by the loose kaftan. Kitty began to make the effort, slowly and painfully, to rise from her high-seated chair, but before she could do so, Sophie was across the room.

It was as if she'd never been away.

The spate of questions tumbled out, willy-nilly. 'Why did you go away like that? Why did you let me think you were dead? Why wouldn't you let me come and see you when you came back? Kitty, how *could* you?'

Kitty let them run on, then waved her to stop. 'My dearest Sophie, how could I not? I had no choice.'

'No *choice*?'

If the house still exerted its old spell, so could Kitty, the old enchantress, weave the same magic. Though physically old even when Sophie had first known her, she had always seemed ageless and, after those first few moments of shock, was so now. Sophie knelt by the chair and took one of the malformed hands in hers, as gently as she could, so as not to hurt, and lifted it to her cheek. 'Tell me,' she said.

And with a sigh, Kitty, at last, willingly gave in. For fourteen years she had kept her own vow of silence, telling herself that Felix was well able to cope with his guilt: it wasn't something that would worry someone of his arrogance or penetrate his armour of self-assurance. But keeping silent over anything had never come naturally or lightly to her, and now that she was so ancient, she was glad at long last to ease herself of the burden.

'You're going to tell me, aren't you, what happened when Irena was killed?' Sophie prompted.

'Go and sit down where I can look at you.'

Once begun, it was easier than she'd thought it would be . . .

She'd been restless and couldn't sleep after leaving them all downstairs. There were too many worries on her mind, too many memories . . . and then the noise had started. 'Such a racket you were making! People shouting and rushing about . . . eventually I got up to go downstairs and see what it was all about. I was standing at the top of the stairs and I saw. Everything,' she said, 'that happened in the hall below.'

Their eyes met. Unspoken messages passed between them. Sophie, seeing how calm Kitty was, despised herself for beginning to shake. 'Why didn't you say anything to the police? No, don't tell me, I can guess! Partly, anyway. It was because you didn't want the police here, poking around among your things? Irena knew about *them* . . .' Sophie's gaze went round the room, her eyes resting on one after another of the hated, familiar objects. Her flesh crawled. 'I've always thought she did, that it had something to do with her deciding to go away.'

Kitty nodded slowly. 'And you knew, too.'

'I only guessed, but I was sure I must be right. Irena kept throwing out hints. She'd picked up enough knowledge from her father to be able to tell what was genuine from what was fake. And there were other things that made me think, when you were dictating your memoirs . . .' Sophie looked miserable. 'I just put two and two together.'

'Clever Sophie, I used to wonder if you might. Yes, Irena told me she knew they were genuine. Not that the ethics of it bothered her, not in the least. She promised she'd never say a word, on condition that I made her a regular allowance, so that she didn't need to stay here, could go away and pursue her own life as she chose. I thought it was a small price to pay, but in any case, what else could I have done?'

'You couldn't have given them back without bringing Alfred into it and destroying his reputation, I see that. Someone as highly respected as he was, "collecting" them and getting them out of the country.'

Kitty responded sharply to the implicit accusation. 'That was the only reason why I kept them after he died! Well, that and the fact that I would never have been allowed back on any site to work if it had been made known I'd shut my eyes to what he was doing—and what good would that have done anyone? I still had years of valuable work in front of me and—'

'Why?' Sophie interrupted. 'Why did he do it? I can't believe he intended to sell them, though they must be worth a mint.'

'Sell? What can you be thinking of? The reasons were more complicated than that. He was not a well man, in fact he was dying. He'd made plans to end his days at Flowerdew and would have done so if it hadn't been for the accident that killed him. These things had already been despatched. He only wanted to keep a few memories of a lifetime's devotion . . . Was that so very bad?'

Stolen memories, thought Sophie. What were they worth?

'I never quite believed Irena's promise to say nothing. She was not someone you could rely on. But don't think I haven't questioned my part that night, though at the time there was only one thing I could think of—that now, Alfred's reputation would be safe. So I simply turned my back, left you all to it and went back to my room. I heard you all moving about downstairs for a long time and I waited for the police to arrive, for one of you to come and tell me what had happened. But none of you did. So then I knew you'd thought of some sort of cover-up among you. All the same, I couldn't imagine life going on as though nothing had happened . . . knowing what those you trusted are capable of . . . I couldn't face any of you, knowing you were lying to me, knowing that murder had been committed and you were all a party to hiding it from me.' The tremulous self-pitying tears of old age sprang to her eyes. 'I decided to go away, immediately, until I could think what to do. The answer's never been vouchsafed to me, until now.'

'So in the end you stayed away for fourteen years. But you're going to tell the truth now, aren't you, Kitty? To the police?' Sophie spoke to her as if she were a child. 'You'll have to, you know, though I think they know you're involved by now, anyway.'

'Yes, I've accepted that now. When it seemed that Felix was going to get away with it, there seemed no point in letting the truth be known, ruining several lives for the sake of what is called justice. I was prepared to stay silent as long as Irena's death remained unsuspected, but not now. I can't go on letting Felix take the blame for a murder he didn't commit.'

'What are you talking about?'

'Felix did not murder Irena Bron.'

Silence. 'Kitty,' Sophie said, 'Kitty dear, Felix *did* kill her—he didn't mean to, perhaps, but he lost his temper and strangled her. He killed her, there was no question about it, she was *dead*!' She gave a great shudder, her eyes enormous. 'We helped, all of us, to—to get rid of her body.' She was almost faint for a moment at the memory of what they'd had to do, and another recollection, perhaps worse, of Angie's little, scrabbling hands, pulling off Irena's ear-rings and stuffing them into her pocket. Angie, who could have bought them a thousand times over!

'Yes, Sophie, I know she was dead,' Kitty said, 'but Felix didn't kill her—though I dare say it was only by pure chance that he didn't!'

'Then how was it,' Sophie said, her voice rising in spite of herself, 'that when I came into the hall, her body was lying there, dead. Tommo saw her as well—he came back with Felix from the car as I came into the hall—and I tell you she was *dead*!'

'While he was out, fetching Madeleine's bag from her car, I saw Irena stir, heard her groan. And I saw what happened next.' Kitty's eyes strayed to the tape-recorder on her desk. 'It's all there, Sophie. All of it. Jessie guessed there was something troubling me, years ago, and she bullied me until I put it all on tape. It's just as well to prepare for any eventuality when you get to my age. I shall see that it's given to the police.'

CHAPTER 21

Madeleine Freeman, driving her Volvo up Hill Street, saw the lights shining from the windows of the old chapel some time before she noticed the phalanx of cars parked alongside the pavement and inside the forecourt.

She peered along the dimly-lit road, puzzled at first. It wasn't one of the nights when any of the campaigners should have been working there; it was Tuesday, the same night of the week that Angie had died. Then she saw the cars were police cars and her heart began to hammer against her ribcage with a painful, irregular rhythm.

The police, what are the police doing *there*? Not to worry, they won't find anything. The mac. Oh God, the plastic mac! Don't panic, they won't look in every single cupboard —and if they do, what will a plastic mac mean to them? All the same, I should have got rid of it—what in heaven's name made me forget?

She went on, up the hill. Although she was accustomed to driving in the dark, she had never liked it. The last time she'd been forced to do it, Angie had been sitting beside her. Now she drove erratically, grinding the gears and braking too sharply at traffic lights and zebra crossings.

Don't panic. There's nothing to have told them Angie was at the chapel that night—there was very little struggle, she went like a lamb to the slaughter. Until the very last moment, when she realized what was happening and her eyes bulged with terror and she went frantic and tried to pull my hands away. But she had no chance. It was almost too easy: '*Angie, darling, life's too short to keep up this sort of silly quarrel. My marrying Edward needn't make any difference to us. Make up and be friends again?*' Arms held out for a hug, Angie walking into them. Dead, two minutes later. No more trouble, get on with my life, the millstone that's been round my neck gone for ever. It was a choice, my life or hers, and whose is of the most value to the community?

They had found the plastic mac, complete with a tear in the sleeve. It had been stuffed where hymn books had once been stored, inside the lift-up seat of one of the varnished pew-benches set round the walls of the small meeting-room off the main vestibule, a room once used for Sunday school classes and now the main campaign office. The walls were adorned with familiar posters. Piles of leaflets stood about

on the floor and on the trestle-tables serving as desks.
A first-generation word processor and printer occupied
another and an ancient photocopier stood in the corner.
The white-overalled SOCO team had almost finished;
Dexter was labelling the contents of a small plastic envelope
and a young woman was sticky-taping the doorframe for
latent fingerprints. Dexter said laconically, 'This might be
of interest to you,' and held out the envelope, inside which
were two fragments of red-varnished fingernail.

All in all, precious little.

Madeleine drove home, or the place she was still forced to
call home for the moment, the hated house on Kilbracken
Road—strangely, even more hateful now that it was empty
of Angie. She was still there, in every room, round every
corner. I miss you, Angie, it hurts like a phantom limb
that's been amputated, in spite of all those years of hating
you and wishing you dead a thousand times. But even
death, it seems, hasn't been able to break the bond between
us, that love/hate relationship going right back to when we
were at school.

I was always conscious of you there, on the edges of the
group of girls who were my set. I was their leader, popular,
pretty and clever, a favourite with the teachers. None of
them guessed how poor I really was, and what untold mis-
ery my life at home held. I was too proud to tell anyone
about my father beating me, I hid the bruises along with
the determination that I was going to get out from under,
come what may. You had no need for such subterfuges, but
you were never liked. You were always ready to take offence
at imagined slights . . . You had a malicious tongue and
the other girls were a little bit afraid of you. And yet I used
to pretend I was you, a rich little girl with a doting father.
Sometimes I almost believed it was true. Perhaps that was
why I let you hang around, though I came to hate your
scarred face and your spiteful nature. You had your uses,

though: the other girls admired me because they thought I was being kind to you—and you were willing to share your oodles of pocket money and your new bicycle.

There were other things you later forced me to share . . . this house—and even the one thing I could truly call my own: my work to keep the Women's Hospital open. But you'd been growing tiresome long before that. I was already looking round for ways to rid myself of you when it happened . . .

You never said a word about what you'd seen, but we both knew. From then on there was no escape for me. I was bound to you. You were my shadow, my Nemesis . . .

Why were the police at Hill Street chapel? They must suspect something. Where have I made my mistakes? So far, everything's gone my way, even things I couldn't have planned for or foreseen . . . though I have planned. All those years I was conscious that Felix Darbell was the unpredictable factor. I couldn't know which way he might jump. It cost me money to have him watched, to keep myself up to date with his life and circumstances, but it was worth it in the end. I was able to find out where he was when I needed him. And it wasn't simply luck that he kept that rendezvous in Bulstrode Street . . . I would have staked my life that he would go there after seeing that manuscript I had written, though I couldn't have known he would speak to Mrs Kitchener. That was a piece of luck I couldn't have anticipated.

The doorbell.

There was suddenly a clamour of panic inside her head, battering at her so that her skull felt fit to split in two. For several indecisive moments she stood immobile, then her natural confidence asserted itself.

Two of them stood there, the Chief Inspector and the bouncy-looking woman sergeant with the thick plait.

'A few questions, Dr Freeman. It won't take long.'

'What questions?' *Try not to sound so defensive. Smile.* 'Come in, please. Would you like some coffee?'

'No, thank you.' The sergeant sounded unhelpful, as she and the Chief Inspector came into the room.

They sat stiffly on the edges of their chairs and Mayo said, 'Can you remember exactly what time you came home last Tuesday evening?'

'Yes, straight after surgery. It finished at seven, so I'd be home by about ten past.'

'Are you sure, Dr Freeman?'

'Absolutely.'

'And you didn't go out again until you went out to dinner with Mr Bouvier at eight-fifteen?'

'No.'

'I should tell you that we have evidence you were not here at eight o'clock.'

How did they know that? Somebody rang and got my answering service? Somebody called? Felix? 'I was probably having my bath and didn't hear.'

He made no comment on this, but asked, 'Do you own this plastic mackintosh?'

Sealed in a labelled plastic bag, it was produced from the sergeant's leather shoulder-bag. 'Certainly not.'

'It was found in a cupboard at the Hill Street chapel, which you use as your campaign headquarters.'

'Well, I'm not the only one using that place, am I?'

'I must also tell you that our forensic people have found pieces of fingernail there, which we believe to be Angie Robinson's. We believe that she met her death there.' And suddenly, 'Did you kill Angie Robinson, Dr Freeman?'

She despised alcohol as a prop, but she could have done with a drink at that moment. Even a drink of water, her mouth was so dry. She licked her lips and said, 'I find that a very offensive remark. I am a doctor, dedicated to saving life, not taking it, especially that of my dearest friend.'

There was an expression on his face she could not read,

a dark look, flared nostrils. Was it contempt? 'Please get your coat, Dr Freeman. I think we should be well advised to continue this interview down at Milford Road police station.'

'You can't do this to me, you've nothing against me!'

'I'm arresting you on suspicion of the wilful murder of Irena Bron.'

She felt the adrenalin draining from her extremities. Her facial muscles seemed to have stiffened so that she found it difficult to speak. '*Irena Bron?* That's ridiculous. You already have the man who murdered her. Felix Darbell has confessed!'

'Because Felix Darbell genuinely thought he had killed her. And it wasn't for want of trying—but when you knelt down beside her and saw she was still alive, it was you who put your hands round her throat and finished her off.'

'This is pure supposition!'

'Rather more than that. We have a witness.'

'No, she's—'

'Dead? Were you going to say? Killed because she saw you do it? Yes, I think Angie Robinson did see what happened. I think she was killed because she knew what you'd done and was threatening to tell what she'd seen. But the witness I'm talking about isn't Angie Robinson. There was someone else who saw what you did. Mrs Wilbraham was at the top of the stairs and we have her testimony as to what happened.'

'Why did you kill Irena Bron, Dr Freeman?'

'She was very nearly dead when I got into the hall.' Her voice was strong. The drive to the police station had given her time to get herself together. She was defiant and ready, almost eager, to confess. Like many another confession Mayo had heard, it was laced with bravado and a determination not to see herself in the wrong. 'So nearly dead it was a kindness to do what I did. Do you realize that if she had lived, she might have been paralysed, even brain-damaged?'

'Kindness!' Mayo repeated. He felt he'd heard it all now. 'And you say you're dedicated to saving life, not taking it! In my experience, doctors don't accept defeat so easily. So why did you really do it?'

She saw it was useless and gave up any pretence at virtue. 'Why?' she repeated, almost viciously. 'Because Kitty Wilbraham had promised me money for the Women's Hospital. I was trying at that time to get it privately funded and she'd promised me a very substantial donation and to leave the rest to the fund when she died. Then Irena came on the scene . . . Kitty's daughter.'

'What made you think Mrs Wilbraham was her mother?'

'It was obvious, as Felix pointed out to me, and why else would Kitty have taken her in—and made her an allowance when she decided to go away? Irena told me that much herself, and hinted there was more to come. At any rate there wasn't going to be much left for me, for the hospital. I was devastated but there wasn't much I could do about it—until I saw her lying there on the floor, seconds away from death. I knew exactly what I had to do. In a split second it came to me that I could so easily make everything what it was before . . . I had no idea Kitty had seen.' But the small frown showed only displeasure; not the faintest shadow of remorse or guilt.

'Did you not suspect when she went away so suddenly?'

'Kitty was always capricious—and I had enough problems of my own to think about. It simply didn't occur to me.'

He thought perhaps it hadn't. She was so essentially self-orientated, she would be able to block out all issues other than the one which was of immediate concern to her. 'And your main problem was, of course, Angie Robinson, who had also seen what happened.'

But if she had been ready enough, in the face of Kitty Wilbraham's taped evidence, to admit to killing Irena Bron, the murder of Angie Robinson was a different matter. What he needed here, too, was a confession. He had a feeling he wasn't going to get it. She sat quite motionless, but her eyes were shadowed and the little frown between her brows had become a deep cleft. She lifted her chin defiantly and stared out of the murky window of the interview room.

'I think Angie Robinson had been blackmailing you emotionally ever since that time. She kept your secret, but her silence was dearly bought. Obligation, someone once said, is a pain, and I think you saw your forthcoming marriage with Mr Bouvier as a way out. But there lay your mistake.' Her hands clenched and she blinked rapidly behind her spectacles and he thought for a moment he'd got to her. 'It was the one thing Angie would never have tolerated, and everything stemmed from that. I believe she threatened you with exposure if you didn't call off the wedding. Perhaps she'd also threatened to write to us? Or told you she had, but naming no names?'

She gave him no help, and he resumed patiently, 'You were not, I think, certain whether she'd sent that letter until I told you about it, but you must have known that if she had, sooner or later we would come round to the events at Flowerdew. And that was why you decided to kill her and set Felix Darbell up for it.'

He stopped, letting the silence go on until at last, unable to resist, she said drily, 'I congratulate you on your imagination, Chief Inspector, but that's absolutely all it is.'

'I don't think so. You made sure we got on to Felix Darbell by dropping his name to me. There were witnesses to prove he'd committed one murder—he believed it himself. If you could make it seem as though Angie had been blackmailing him over this, it would provide a reason for her murder.

'But you had to get him here, to Lavenstock, and put him in a position where he could be blamed. So you constructed an elaborate charade which would ensure he was at Bulstrode Street at eight o'clock that night. Meanwhile, you had enticed Angie from her flat and down to the old chapel by means of a phone call—some pretext to do with your campaign, no doubt. It was a very convenient place for you, being in close proximity both to where you lived and the hospital car park where you could later leave her car. And, being Tuesday night, you could count on not being disturbed. While she was on her way, you used your key to slip quietly into her flat and leave a note for Felix Darbell asking him to wait, providing whisky and a glass for him while he waited, and then drove to meet Angie at the chapel. I suggest that by the time Mr Darbell got to her flat, Angie Robinson had been strangled and her body was on its way, in her own car, to Hartopp Moor. All you had to do then was to park the Astra, return to the flat to remove the note and to lock the door and get back to Kilbracken Road in time to dine out with Mr Bouvier. The timing was tight, but you managed it.'

There was silence when he had finished. She sat looking at her clasped hands on the table in front of her.

He said conversationally, 'It's ironic, you know. The one thing I admired most in you was the thing that gave you away. I saw you as an idealist, Dr Freeman, someone essentially honest—' her eyes slid towards him—'and then I learned that you didn't own the house on Kilbracken Road, as you'd led us to believe. A harmless enough little deception in itself, and what did it matter? It made a better story, put you in a favourable light—and that's very important to you, isn't it? But it set me wondering whether you'd been entirely truthful about everything . . . We began to look into other things you'd told us, and we found that Angie was far from being the abused and under-privileged child you had made her out to be, whereas a little girl called Madeleine Freeman—'

'Stop it! You can't have any idea how it was!'

*

'After that, there was no holding her. She made a full confession to both murders.' And once started, she had insisted
on every detail being correct, mostly in order to justify
herself, but also to prove her own cleverness. An exercise
in self-aggrandisement.

Mayo stretched his feet towards the roaring log flames.
The small table was set in the inglenook beside the great
stone fireplace of the old inn. On the table was an enormous
pot of tea, a healthy-sized pile of buttered toast, some scones
and homemade raspberry jam. Alex was seated opposite,
her normally pale skin glowing from exercise and cold and
the ruddy light of the fire. They'd just walked seven bracing
miles across country on the last cold, sunny afternoon in
March, a day full of spring promise. Walked for the most
part in silence, enjoying the luxury of each other's company
and, for Mayo at least, the release of pressure after the
winding up of the Angie Robinson case.

He hadn't spoken much about it to Alex during the major
part of the investigation or while the later, supplementary
inquiries were being carried out, but now, when all that
remained was to deal with the paperwork and the legal
formalities necessary to prepare a case for prosecution,
she'd known he'd feel the need to talk and get the case out
of his system. There were still weeks of work ahead, but all
routine stuff. The worst of the pressure had been lifted and
he could relax and feel at ease.

'I still find it incredible, the thought of someone like
Madeleine Freeman committing two deliberate murders,'
she said.

A public personality, and so dedicated, hard-working
and caring, she had seemed—but somehow gone wrong,
marred by some fatal flaw. Angie Robinson might have
been scarred but so was Madeleine. In her case, marked
from an early age by something other than a visible scar.

'It's a matter of losing control,' Mayo said. 'Once she
did, she was prepared to go to any lengths, even to incrimi-

nate an innocent man. Not just any man, but one who'd already borne the burden of her guilt for fourteen years. Do you know what she said to that? *"It was unfortunate that suspicion should have to fall on Felix, but I had to think of my career, my work."* '

'Does she feel no guilt?'

'None at all, I'm convinced. She'd have killed anyone who got in her way, without any compunction.'

He finished the last scone and his third cup of tea. 'Any more in the pot?'

She squeezed out another cup, and added hot water to the pot. It was dim and cosy here by the fire. The pungently-scented logs settled in a rosy glow. He smiled at her. He thought she looked beautiful in her soft, rust-coloured sweater, a silk scarf at her neck and tan trousers tucked into gleaming leather boots.

During their walk they had passed the tumbledown little house Abigail had set her heart on. 'Well, it has character,' Mayo said, looking hard at the roof and the spoutings and the surrounding jungle that was the garden. 'If nothing else.'

'She'll cope.'

'Oh, I've do doubt!' He grinned, then said casually, 'Alone?'

'Alone.' They continued along the path and Alex said, 'She's off men, for the moment. They don't mix with ambition.'

'She might find there's more to life than ambition.'

This was dangerous ground and she hadn't replied. Had he guessed at the still unresolved questions churning around in her mind? Perhaps he had, for he'd changed the subject: 'There's something about these old houses and the way they reflect their owners. Take that place, Flowerdew —and Mrs Wilbraham. I went back there to get her signed testimony and she seems to have taken on a new lease of life. She's talking about having the chimneys seen to and the house redecorated! She's a cunning old bird . . . I don't believe she's told us everything there is to know about Irena Bron's murder, any more than Madeleine Freeman has . . . but to prosecute a woman of her age? What else is there to do but turn a blind eye, to that and whatever else she's done?' He added, apparently inconsequentially, 'She told me she's going to leave what's left of her money, and all those artefacts that are in her red room, to the Bardo museum in Tunis.'

'I thought they were replicas?'

'Then they won't accept them, will they?' His expression was enigmatic.

'You put it admirably.'

She was still thinking about what he'd said as they went outside into the darkening afternoon. The sun was going down over the hill, beyond which lay Flowerdew, far to the left. 'Was Irena Bron Kitty's daughter?' she asked.

'Who knows now, except Kitty herself?'

It didn't matter. There were always unresolved questions, doubts and dissatisfactions. No case was ever as complete as he would like. They still had another two miles to walk to get back to where they'd left the car. There was no hurry but now that the sun had gone down the wind was cold. He reached out for her hand and they set off briskly down the village street.